THE AUTHOR: Natsume Sōseki was bo[...] 1867. After graduating from Tokyo Imperial U[...] [whe]re he majored in English literature, he became [...] [t]he rural island of Shikoku, and a year later he [...] [Ky]ushu, the southern island, where he taught at a [...] [I]n 1900 he was sent to England on a government [...] [schol]arship, and he remained there until 1903; it was [...] [y]ears abroad that he developed a nervous disor[der...] [plagu]ed him for the rest of his life. In 1905 he publish[ed ...] [wor]k of fiction, *Wagahai wa neko de aru*, followed by t[he ...] [C]han, *Kusamakura*, and *Nihyaku tōka*, which established h[im ...] [as a] creative writer of major importance. The light-hearted satir[ic]al tone of some of these early works gave way, however, to the seriousness of *Kōfu*, *Sanshirō*, and *Sore kara*. Despite bouts of acute illness, Sōseki's literary output during his last decade included *Mon*, *Kōjin*, and *Kokoro*, and culminated in the unfinished novel, *Meian*—a study of alienation and loneliness. He died in 1916.

BOTCHAN

Natsume Sōseki

Translated by
Alan Turney

KODANSHA INTERNATIONAL
Tokyo and New York

This translation was originally commissioned by the Japanese National Commission for UNESCO.

Illustrations by Hosokibara Seiki (1885–1958)

Distributed in the United States by Kodansha International/USA Ltd., 114 Fifth Avenue, New York, New York 10011. Published by Kodansha International Ltd., 17-14, Otowa 1-chome, Bunkyo-ku, Tokyo 112 and Kodansha International/USA, Ltd. Copyright © 1972 by Kodansha International Ltd. All rights reserved. Printed in Japan.

LCC 71-174215
ISBN 0-87011-367-4
ISBN 4-7700-0701-9 (in Japan)

First edition, 1972
First paperback edition, 1978
Twelfth printing, 1990

INTRODUCTION

Natsume Kinnosuke, who is generally referred to by his pen name Sōseki, was born in 1867, one year before the Meiji Restoration. The Meiji period was one of flux in all areas of culture, for it saw Japan's sluice gates opened to admit a flood of Western ideas. Nowhere was this state of flux more apparent than in the field of literature.

Sōseki's first contact with a literature other than Japanese seems to have been in 1881 when, at the age of fourteen, he studied Chinese literature for a year at school. His love of Chinese literature stayed with him throughout his life, and its influence can sometimes be seen in his works.

In 1882 Sōseki expressed a wish to make literature his career, although not specifying whether as a writer or a scholar. However, his eldest brother discouraged him. Nevertheless, Sōseki entered the Department of English Literature of Tokyo Imperial University in 1890.

During the Meiji period, Japan's intelligentsia considered it their duty to study things Western in order to help the development of their country. Sōseki was no exception, and it was a desire to gain a knowledge of one of the cultural aspects of Western civilization that lead him to undertake the study of English literature.

Sōseki had no intention of deserting Chinese literature in favor of its Western counterpart. Moreover, he did not regard what he was doing as "changing" at all. In his own estimation he was only extending his studies to another facet of that phenomenon which he had studied and loved for many years—literature. Differences, of course, he expected, but he believed that essentially Chinese and English literature were only two sides of the same coin. His realization that they were radically different only developed very slowly and did not reach fruition until he was in London about ten years later. With this realization came a disappointment in English literature.

In 1895 Sōseki graduated from the Imperial University and went as a teacher of English to the Matsuyama Middle School in Shikoku. This later became the setting for *Botchan*. After a year in Matsuyama, Sōseki moved to another post in Kyushu. He remained there for four years until 1900 when the Ministry of Education sent him to England for two years as a research scholar.

Up to and including his time in England, Sōseki may be considered more a scholar than a writer, although he did write many Chinese poems and *haiku* (the latter as a result of his friendship at the university with Masaoka Shiki, who was the greatest name in the revival of *haiku* poetry at that period). After Sōseki returned to Japan, however, he turned to the writing of novels, while continuing for a time his pursuit of scholarship, and went on to become one of the greatest writers in Japanese literature.

Sōseki's first novel was a social satire entitled *Wagahai wa Neko de Aru* (I Am a Cat). This was published in 1905. Encouraged by the great success of this work,

Sōseki published his second novel, *Botchan*, in 1906. This book too was extremely popular, and has continued to be a great favorite with Japanese readers.

The word *botchan* is untranslatable because of the many nuances it contains. It is basically a form of polite address used to the sons, generally while they are children, of well-to-do families. It is akin to the rather archaic English phrase "the young master." Yet, being a diminutive, it carries a nuance of affection not contained in the English. On occasion, the word may also imply that the person so referred to is, because of his background, rather spoiled and self-willed. The main reason that Sōseki dubbed the protagonist of this novel Botchan, however, is that he was trying to convey the deep feelings of affection and loyalty which the old servant, Kiyo, had for him.

To the Western reader, the story line of this novel may appear rather thin, and he may find himself wondering wherein its attraction lies for the Japanese. Certainly the story has little point. It is also true that the humor is dated. But the book does retain a great appeal for Japanese people. Part of this attraction lies in the cavalier attitude with which Botchan breezes from one catastrophe to another. He is no respecter of person or convention, and this endears him as much to modern Japanese as it did to readers sixty-odd years ago, because even today a Japanese can feel himself hedged in by social niceties.

Perhaps the greatest appeal that *Botchan* has for readers nowadays is a nostalgic one. The feeling evoked in the Japanese reader is similar to that evoked in an Englishman or American reading a description of a Victorian Christmas by Charles Dickens.

7

Botchan has been dramatized, particularly for television, many times. It is most often shown during the summer, and there is something about the atmosphere which pervades this work that is as in tune with a Japanese summer as *Chūshingura* is with a Japanese winter.

One problem I faced in translating this book is that Tokyoites, of whom Botchan is one, have a propensity for making puns. The problem is not merely that it is difficult to find a comparable pun in English, but that puns in English are very rarely funny. Another problem is that some of the characters in this book speak in a very distinctive dialect—in one place a pun is made in dialect. I have done my best to deal with these problems, but I am aware that the result is far from ideal.

Botchan is said to have been Sōseki's favorite novel and occupies an important place in Japanese literature. I hope that my English rendition has captured the atmosphere of the original sufficiently to give to foreign readers, if not the sense of nostalgia experienced by their Japanese counterparts, at least some inkling of the Japanese taste in literature.

Alan Turney

Tokyo, October 1971

1

Ever since I was a child, my inherent recklessness has brought me nothing but trouble.

Once, when I was at primary school, I jumped out of a second-story window and couldn't walk for a week. Some of you may be wondering why I did such a rash thing. There was no particularly deep reason. It was just that, as I stuck my head out of a second-floor window of the new block, one of my classmates jeered at me and said, "You're always bragging, but I bet you couldn't jump from there. Yah! Sissy!"

When I arrived home on the caretaker's back, my father glared at me and said, "Whoever heard of anyone shaking at the knees after only jumping from the second floor?" To which I replied that I'd show him. Next time they wouldn't shake.

A relation of mine had given me a foreign-made pen-knife, and I was holding up the beautiful blade to show my friends how it caught the sunlight when one of them said, "It shines, all right, but I bet it won't cut."

"What do you mean, won't cut? It'll cut anything," I replied, accepting the challenge.

"All right then, let's see you cut your finger," he demanded.

"A finger? Huh! It'll cut a finger as easy as this." So saying, I cut diagonally into the back of my right thumb. Fortunately, it was a small knife, and the bone was hard, so I still have my thumb. But the scar will be with me for life.

If you walked the twenty paces to the eastern end of our

garden, you came to a small vegetable plot on a southern slope, right in the middle of which stood a chestnut tree. This tree meant more to me than life itself. When the nuts were ripe, I would go out the back door as soon as I got up, collect those that lay on the ground, and eat them at school. The west side of the vegetable plot adjoined the garden of the Yamashiroya pawnshop, where there lived a kid of thirteen or fourteen called Kantarō. Kantarō was, of course, a coward. But, in spite of this, he used to climb over the trellis fence and steal the chestnuts.

One evening I hid in the shadow of the gate and caught him at last. Having lost his way of escape, he flung himself at me with all his force. He was about two years older than me and, although he was a coward, he was strong. As he made a sudden lunge at my chest with his flat-crowned head, it skidded off into the sleeve of my kimono. Since this prevented me from using my hand, I swung my arm about blindly. Kantarō's head, trapped in my sleeve, whipped giddily to left and right. Finally, being in pain, he clamped his teeth onto my upper arm inside the sleeve. This hurt, so I pushed him up against the fence and threw him backwards with a leg trip. The ground on the pawn-shop side was about six feet lower than the vegetable plot. Kantarō, smashing down half the trellis in the process, fell headfirst back into his own territory and landed with a groan. As he fell, one of the sleeves of my kimono was torn off and my hand suddenly came free. That evening my mother went across to apologize and, while she was there, retrieved my sleeve.

I got into many other kinds of mischief besides this. For instance, there was the time when I ruined Mosaku's carrot patch with good old Kane, who worked for the local carpenter, and Kaku, the fishmonger's boy. An area where the sprouts had not come out evenly had been covered with straw, so we spent half a day having wrestling matches on it, and trampled all the carrots.

10

As he made a sudden lunge at my chest with his flat-crowned head, it skidded off into the sleeve of my kimono.

Another time I caught it in the neck for blocking up the well in Furukawa's rice field. This was a device whereby water welled up and out onto the surrounding rice plants through a thick piece of bamboo which had been sunk deep into the ground, after first having had its joints pierced to make it into a hollow tube. At the time I didn't know what kind of device it was, and so stuffed sticks and stones down it. Having made sure that the flow of water had stopped, I went home, and was having a meal, when Furukawa came roaring in with a face as red as a beet. As I remember, money had to change hands before the matter was settled.

My father never showed me the slightest affection, and my mother always favored my elder brother. He was terribly white-skinned and liked to pretend he was an actor, taking the female parts. Every time my father looked at me, he used to say, "He'll never amount to anything." And my mother used to say, "He's so rough and unruly, I worry what'll become of him." In fact, I never *have* amounted to anything. You can see the result for yourself. It's no wonder they were worried what would become of me. The only thing that can be said to my credit is that I have gone through life—so far—without getting put into penal servitude.

My mother was ill, and two or three days before she died I was turning somersaults in the kitchen and banged my ribs very painfully on the corner of the cooking stove. My mother was very angry and said she never wanted to see my face again, so I went to stay with relatives. At last the news came that she had died. I didn't think she'd die so soon. I came home thinking that if I'd known she was that seriously ill, I'd have been a little quieter. Then my brother said that I was a bad son, and that it was because of me that our mother died when she did. I was terribly upset and slapped him across the face, for which I got into a great deal of trouble.

After my mother died, I lived with my father and brother. My father was the kind of man who did nothing, and who would only have to catch sight of your face to come out with, "You're useless! Useless!" It was like a habit with him, but I still don't know what he was referring to. There's no two ways about it, I had a strange father.

My brother said he was going into business, and spent all his time studying English. He had always had a womanish disposition and, since he was also a sneak, we weren't on good terms. We had a row, on average, about once a week. Once, when we were playing Japanese chess, he made a sneaky move and looked very pleased with himself as he made fun of the position I was in. I was so annoyed that I flung the rook I was holding at his head. It caught him between the eyes, broke the skin, and drew a little blood. He went and told my father, who said that he disowned me.

I knew that there was nothing I could do about it and so considered myself disowned as my father had said, but Kiyo, who had been our maid for ten years, went to him in tears and begged him to forgive me, until eventually his anger subsided. Nevertheless, I was not particularly frightened of my father. Strangely enough, it was Kiyo I felt sorry for.

I had heard that Kiyo came from a good family, but that when they were ruined, she had been reduced at last to going into service. That's why she was now an old woman and not an elderly lady. I don't know why, but this old woman was extremely kind to me. It was very strange. My mother, three days before she died, had given up all hope for me; my father found me unmanageable the whole year round; and the people in our area looked down on me as a rough urchin—yet Kiyo, blind to all this, thought I was wonderful. I had resigned myself to the fact that I was definitely not the kind of person that people liked, and so thought nothing of it when they treated me like dirt.

13

As a matter of fact, it was Kiyo's dancing attendance on me that made me suspicious.

Sometimes, in the kitchen, when no one else was about, Kiyo would say, "You're straightforward, and you have a nice nature." But I didn't know what she meant. If that were the case, why didn't other people besides Kiyo treat me well, too. When Kiyo said things like that, I usually answered that I hated flattery, whereupon she would say, "There, you see. You *do* have a nice nature," and would gaze at me happily. It was as though she took pride in me because she had created me herself. It was weird.

When my mother died, Kiyo began to show me even more affection. At times my child's mind would be suspicious and wonder why she was so kind. I didn't like it and wished she would stop. I felt sorry for her. Nevertheless, she continued to fuss over me. Sometimes she would buy me, out of her own money, Kintsuba cakes shaped like sword-guards, or Kōbaiyaki biscuits in the form of plum blossoms. She would quietly buy some flour and set it aside, and then, on cold nights, without saying anything she would bring me some noodle soup as I lay in bed. There were times when she would even buy me a bowl of noodles with vegetables.

Her presents didn't stop at food. She bought me socks, pencils, notebooks and once, though this was much later, even lent me three yen. I didn't ask for it. She brought the money to my room and said, "You can't get along without pocket-money. Here, take this." Of course I said I didn't want it, but, since she insisted, I took it. To tell the truth, I was very glad.

I put the three yen in my purse, and the purse into the breast of my kimono; but then when I went to the lavatory, it disappeared down the hole. There was nothing I could do about it, so I crept out and told Kiyo what had happened. She said straight away that she would go and look for a bamboo pole and get the money back for me.

After a while, I heard the sound of running water near the well, and when I went out to look, there was Kiyo washing the purse, which she had dangling by its string from the end of the bamboo. Afterwards she opened the purse and examined the one-yen notes. They had turned brown and the pattern was beginning to fade. Kiyo dried them by our charcoal brazier and held them out to me, saying that they were all right now. I sniffed at them a little and said that they smelled, so Kiyo said, "All right, give them here. I'll go and change them for you."

I don't know where she went or who she tricked to do it, but she came back with the three yen in silver coins. I've forgotten what I spent that three yen on. I told her that I'd pay her back soon, but I never did. And now I can't, even though I wish I could, ten times over.

Kiyo only gave me things when neither my father nor brother were there. I told her that there was nothing I disliked more than receiving things on the sly, by myself. Of course I didn't get on with my brother, but I didn't want cakes or crayons from Kiyo behind his back. When I asked Kiyo why she only gave things to me and not my brother, she answered, completely unperturbed, that it was all right because my father bought things for him. This was unfair, for although he was stubborn, he was not given to favoritism. But I suppose that's the way it looked to Kiyo, since she was obviously infatuated. This kind of attitude couldn't be helped, because, although she originally came from a good family, she was just an uneducated old woman. Her partiality, however, went farther than this. It was, in fact, frightening. She was convinced that someone like me would get on in life and become a great man, but that my brother, who was always studying, was good for nothing, in spite of his fair, patrician skin. She was beyond me. If she liked you, you would be a success; if she didn't, you were going to be a miserable failure. Although I couldn't see myself becoming anything, Kiyo

15

kept on saying, "You will! You will!", so I thought that perhaps I might after all. Looking back on it all now, it seems ridiculous. I once asked Kiyo what I was going to be, but even she had no special idea beyond the fact that I would undoubtedly ride in my own private rickshaw and build a house with a fine entrance.

Kiyo wanted to come with me when I had my own house and became independent, and repeatedly asked me if she could. Since I, too, somehow felt that I would have my own house, I said, "Yes, all right," and would have left it at that, but Kiyo had a strong imagination and freely made plans by herself.

"Where would you like to live in Tokyo—Kōjimachi or Azabu?" . . . "Do have a swing made in the garden." . . . "I think one Western-style room will be plenty." These were some of the things to which I had to listen. At the time I didn't have the slightest desire for a house, and I always answered Kiyo that I didn't want one, since neither a Western nor a Japanese house was of any use to me. To this she would reply, "You're unselfish, and you're a good boy." She praised me whatever I said.

This, then, was my life for the first five or six years after my mother died: getting into trouble with my father, quarreling with my brother, and having cakes bought for me, and sometimes being praised, by Kiyo. There was nothing I particularly wanted. I was content with things as they were and thought that that was how most other children lived too. Kiyo, however, kept on telling me that I was a poor boy, and that I was unfortunate, so I came to think that perhaps I was. Apart from that, however, I had nothing to worry me at all—though it did annoy me that my father didn't give me any pocket-money.

In January of the sixth year after my mother died, my father died too, of apoplexy. In April of the same year, I graduated from the private middle school I'd been attending and, in June, my brother graduated from business school. He said he'd had an offer from the Kyushu branch office of some company or other, and that he had to go down there. I still had to study in Tokyo. My brother said he was going to sell the house, dispose of the property and leave. I told him he could do as he pleased. In any case, I had no desire to be under any obligation to him. Even if he looked after me, I knew we'd quarrel. And, if we did, he wouldn't hesitate to remind me how much he was doing for me. So rather than bow and scrape to him for his half-hearted charity, I resolved to look after myself, even if I had to deliver milk to do it.

This settled, my brother called in a second-hand dealer and sold the rubbish of our forefathers for next to nothing. The house itself and the land it stood on were made over to a rich man to whom somebody had kindly introduced us. This, apparently, realized a great deal of money, though I don't know any of the details because I had been in lodgings in Ogawamachi in Kanda for the month before this, waiting to see what was going to happen.

Kiyo was very sad to see the house she had lived in for ten years pass into a stranger's hands, but since it wasn't hers, there was nothing she could do about it. She kept trying to persuade me that if I had been a little older, I would have inherited the house. If that were the case, I ought to inherit it anyway. Kiyo knew nothing about the subject and thought the only thing preventing me from getting my brother's house was my age.

Thus my brother and I parted. But the problem of where Kiyo should go still remained. My brother, of course, was in no position to take her with him, and besides, Kiyo had no wish whatsoever to go traipsing all the way down to Kyushu after him. I was cooped up in a nine-by-nine room in a cheap lodging house, and might have to leave even that if things came to a pinch. Neither of us, then, could help her.

I spoke to Kiyo about the situation and asked her if she

wanted to go into service with some other family. She eventually made up her mind and replied that, since she couldn't come with me until I had a house of my own and was married, she would go and live with her nephew temporarily. This nephew was a clerk in the court and, having always been comfortably off, had two or three times urged Kiyo to come and live with him if she felt so inclined. She had always refused, saying that she preferred living in the house she had grown accustomed to over the years, even if it meant being a maid. But in the present circumstances, I suppose, she had decided it would be better to live with her nephew than to change her job and again go unnecessarily through that period of feeling ill at ease which a new position would mean. She told me, however, to get myself a wife and buy a house quickly, and that she would then come and look after me. It seemed that she liked me, an outsider, better than her own relations.

Two days before he left for Kyushu, my brother came to my lodgings and, handing me six hundred yen, told me that I could use it as capital and go into business, for school expenses if I wanted to study, or in any way I wished, but that I was to expect nothing further from him. This, for my brother, was admirable. It wouldn't have worried me not to have had a lousy six hundred yen, but I was so taken with the unprecedented generosity of this act that I thanked him and accepted the money. My brother handed me another fifty yen and told me to give it to Kiyo, which I readily agreed to do. We parted two days later at Shimbashi station and have never seen each other since.

I lay in bed thinking how I should use the six hundred yen. Running a business was a lot of bother and I wouldn't make a success of it. Besides, it seemed unlikely that you could start up a business worthy of the name on a mere six hundred yen. Even if it were possible, I couldn't, as things stood at the moment, boast to people that I had had an education, which would mean that it would end in

18

failure. Since, therefore, I didn't need capital, I thought I would use the money for school expenses and carry on studying. By using two hundred yen a year, I would be able to study for three years. And, if I worked really hard for those three years, I would be able to achieve something.

I next tried to decide which school I should go to, but I had always disliked one subject as much as another. I particularly wanted no part of languages or literature. I have never been able to understand even one in twenty lines of those modern poems which imitate Western forms and thought. Since I disliked everything, it didn't seem to matter where I studied. Fortunately, however, as I happened to be passing the Tokyo School of Physics one day, I saw a notice announcing vacancies for students and, since this seemed providential, I immediately asked for their prospectus and completed the formalities for entrance. In retrospect, this too seems a blunder caused by my inherent recklessness.

For three years I did an average amount of work, but having no particular aptitude, it was always more convenient to reckon my place in class from the bottom. Strangely enough, however, I was able to graduate. I thought this was curious myself, but since I had no cause for complaint, I held my peace and graduated.

Eight days after graduation, the principal of the school came and asked me to his office, and, thinking that he might have something important to tell me, I went with him. He said that a middle school down in Shikoku needed a mathematics teacher. The salary was forty yen a month, and how about my going there? To tell the truth, although I had studied for three years, I had no wish to become a teacher, nor had I any idea of going to the country. But since I had no idea of becoming anything other than a teacher, I accepted the offer on the spot. Once again that impetuosity with which I was cursed.

Having accepted the offer, I had to leave for my new

post. For the past three years I had confined myself to my nine-by-nine room and had not had to listen to anybody nagging even once. I had also got by without any arguments. This had been a comparatively relaxed period in my life, but now I would have to leave my room. The only time I had ever set foot outside Tokyo was when I had gone on a class outing to Kamakura, only a stone's throw away. This time I had to go a lot farther than Kamakura. On the map, my destination looked no bigger than a pinprick on the coast. It couldn't be much of a place. I didn't know what kind of a town it was, or what kind of people lived there, but that didn't matter. I would just go. I must confess, however, that I found it a bit of a nuisance.

After we had disposed of the house, I had visited Kiyo from time to time. Her nephew turned out to be an unexpectedly fine person. Whenever I went to the house and he was there, he always made me very welcome in every way. Kiyo used to make a lot of me and would tell her nephew the various things about me of which she was proud. She announced that I was soon to graduate and would then buy a large house in the Kōjimachi area, from which I would commute to the government office where I was going to work. Since Kiyo had decided and announced this of her own accord, it put me in a difficult position and I blushed. It wasn't only once or twice that this happened either.

Sometimes she used to embarrass me by bringing up how I used to wet the bed when I was young. I don't know what her nephew must have thought when he listened to her boasting. But Kiyo, being of the old school, regarded our relationship as that of master and retainer during the feudal period. It seemed that, as far as she was concerned, *her* master was, without doubt, the master of her nephew also. What a position for her nephew to be in!

The deal was finally made and, three days before I was due to leave, I went to see Kiyo. She had a cold and was in bed in her six-by-nine room that faced north, but as soon as she saw me she sat up and asked, "Botchan, when are you going to get your house?" She was under the impression that all you had to do was graduate for your pockets to be suddenly filled with money. It really was ridiculous that she should still call someone as eminent as she thought me to be "Botchan." When I told her that buying a house was no easy matter, and wouldn't be for some time yet, and that I was going down into the country, she looked very dejected and smoothed back the disarray of gray-flecked hair along both sides of her head. I felt so sorry for her that, to cheer her up, I said, "I have to go now, but I'll be back soon. I'll definitely come back during the summer holidays next year."

She still looked at me strangely, however, so I said, "I'll buy you a present. What would you like?" She replied that she would like "some of those sweets wrapped in bamboo grass that they have in Echigo." I'd never heard of them and, anyway, Echigo was in the other direction. When I told her that I didn't think they'd have any in the area I was going to, she asked, "Oh? Which direction are you going in?"

"West," I said.

"This side of Hakone or beyond it?" she asked.

Hakone! That's not much farther than Kamakura. What could you do with a woman like that?

On the day of my departure, Kiyo came to see me in the morning and helped me get ready. She had stopped in at the haberdasher's on the way and bought toothpaste, a toothbrush and a towel, which she had put into a canvas bag. I told her that I didn't need anything like that, but she wouldn't listen.

We went to the station side by side in rickshaws, and when we had gone up onto the platform and I had boarded the train, she gazed at my face intently.

"This may be the last time we'll see each other. Take

great care of yourself," she said in a small voice. Her eyes were filled with tears. I didn't cry, but I was on the verge of it. After the train had moved a fairly good distance, I thought it would be all right now and, putting my head out of the window, looked back. She was still standing there. Somehow she looked terribly small.

2

As the boat came to a stop with a deep blast of its siren, a barge pulled away from the shore and made towards us. The lighterman was completely naked, except for a red loincloth. What a barbaric place! Though, of course, nobody could have worn a kimono in that heat. The sun was so strong that its glare on the water dazzled you and made your head swim. I found out from the purser that this was where I got off. The place was a fishing village and looked about the size of the Ōmori area in Tokyo. What a fool they'd taken me for to bring me here! No one could stand a place like this. Still, it was too late now. I was over the side ahead of everybody else and jumped briskly down into the barge, followed by five or six other people. Redpants loaded four large boxes on board and then rowed back for the land.

When we arrived, I was also the first to jump ashore and, grabbing a snotty-nosed kid who was standing there, I asked him where the middle school was. He looked blank and said he didn't know. Dim-witted clod! How could anybody not know where the school was in a pint-sized place like this?

A man wearing a strange kimono with tight-fitting sleeves came up to me and said, "Come this way." I followed him, and he led me to an inn called the Minatoya, or something. Here I was greeted by a group of horrible women chorusing a coy welcome, which rather put me off going in, so I stood at the gate and asked them if they could tell me where the middle school was. They told me that I had to go another two miles by train. This made me even less inclined to go in. I snatched my two bags from the man in the tight-sleeved kimono and crept out, followed by some funny looks from the inn staff.

I soon found the station and bought a ticket without any difficulty. I boarded the train and found that the carriage was about the size of a matchbox. We had only been clattering along for what I judged was about five minutes when I had to get off. No wonder the ticket was so cheap. It only cost three *sen*. I took a rickshaw to the school, but by the time I arrived, classes had already finished and no one was there. The caretaker informed me that the teacher on night duty had just popped out on an errand, which struck me as rather an easy-going attitude for somebody on night duty.

I thought I might call on the headmaster, but since I was tired, I climbed back into the rickshaw and told the coolie to take me to a hotel. He went at a good pace and soon drew up in front of an inn called the Yamashiroya. I was a little amused by the name, because it was the same as that of the pawnshop where Kantarō had lived.

The maid led me to a dark room under the staircase on the second floor. It was intolerably hot. I complained, but she said that unfortunately all the other rooms were taken and, with that, walked off, leaving my bags where she had dumped them. There was nothing for it but to go in and sweat in silence. After a while, they called me and told me that the bath was ready. I went down to the bathroom and had just a quick dip. On the way back to my room, I snooped around and found that there were many rooms empty, all of which looked cool. Ill-mannered lot! Liars!

A little later the maid brought my meal. Although the room was hot, the food was a lot better than it had been in my old lodgings. While the maid was serving, she asked me where I was from, and when I told her "Tokyo," she said, "Tokyo's a nice place, isn't it?"

"Of course it is," I answered.

After she had cleared the dishes away and gone, I heard the sound of loud laughter coming from the direction of the kitchen. I was disgusted by this and went straight to bed, but I just couldn't sleep. Not only was it hot, it was noisy too: about five times as bad as my lodgings.

When at last I did doze off, I dreamed of Kiyo. She was munching Echigo sweets wrapped in bamboo grass, wrapping and all. I told her that she'd better stop, because bamboo grass was poisonous, but she said, no, this was medicine, and really looked as though she were enjoying it. This so took me aback that I opened my mouth and let out a peal of laughter. I woke up with this, to find the maid opening the shutters. It was another brilliant day, without a cloud in the sky.

I had heard that you were expected to tip when you were on a trip, and that, if you didn't, you received bad service. I supposed that it was because I hadn't tipped that they'd shoved me into this small, dark room, and also because I was shabbily dressed, had a canvas bag, and carried an umbrella that was more utilitarian than decorative. What a cheek, looking down on people when they were only peasants themselves! All right, I'd give them something they wouldn't forget in a hurry. In spite of my dress, I had left Tokyo with thirty yen remaining from the money for my school fees, and after train and boat fares and other incidental expenses had been paid, I still had fourteen yen left. I could use all that as a tip, because I would soon be getting my salary. I knew that all country people were tight-fisted, and was sure they'd roll their eyes in surprise at even a five-yen tip. I'll show you, I thought, and went with quiet dignity to wash my face, then returned to my room and waited.

The same maid as on the previous evening brought my breakfast. While she was holding the tray and serving me, she kept grinning in an unpleasant way. Anyone would think I was a freak in a sideshow. Peasant! My face may not be much to look at, but it was a lot better than hers. I had intended to give her the tip when the meal was over, but I was so stung by her behaviour that I handed her a five-yen note while I was still eating and told her to take it down to the front office. She took it with an odd look. When I had finished breakfast, I left for school. They hadn't cleaned my shoes.

Having been to the school in a rickshaw the previous day, I had a good idea where it was. I turned two or three corners and soon came out in front of the gate. The area between the gate and the entrance of the building was paved with granite, and I remembered how the unduly loud rattling as we drove over it the day before had disconcerted me a little. On the way, I met many schoolboys wearing uniforms of the local duck-cloth, who all passed in at this gate. Some of them were taller than me, and looked stronger. The thought that I had to teach them gave me a funny feeling.

I handed over my visiting card, and was shown into the headmaster's room. The headmaster reminded me of a badger, with his sparse side-whiskers, dark skin and big eyes. He was horribly pompous and told me to be diligent and work hard. He then reverently handed me a certificate of appointment, affixed with a large seal. (On my way back to Tokyo, I crumpled this certificate up into a ball and threw it into the sea.) The headmaster said that he would introduce me to the other members of the staff later, and that I was to show the certificate to each of them in turn. What a waste of effort! It would have been better to pin it up in the staff room for three days.

The other teachers wouldn't assemble in the staff room until the bugle sounded for the first period, so I had quite some time to wait. The headmaster pulled out his watch, glanced at it and, saying that he would have a long talk with me later but that first he just wanted me to understand some salient points, proceeded to deliver a lengthy lecture on the spirit of education. I, of course, made a show of listening but, halfway through, decided that I'd made a bad mistake in coming here. I just couldn't behave in the way the headmaster was telling me to. He was asking somebody as wild as I was to set an example for the students, and telling me that I had to be looked up to by the whole school, and that I would never be an educator unless, as an individual, I exerted a good moral influence on the pupils outside school too. This was unreasonable. As if anybody with all those virtues would come all the way out into the country to teach for forty yen a month! I had always thought that all human beings were the same and that they argued if they lost their temper. But if this was the way things were to be, I would scarcely be able to open my mouth, or even go for a stroll. It seemed to me that if the job were as difficult as all that, the facts should have been explained to me before I was taken on.

I hate lies, so I decided to be philosophical about having been tricked into coming here, to speak out and refuse the job, and go back to Tokyo. I had only nine yen in my purse, having given five yen as a tip at the inn, and that wouldn't get me back to Tokyo. I begrudged having given the tip now and wished I hadn't. But even nine yen would be of some use. Even if I didn't have enough money for the fare back, it was better to refuse the job than to tell lies, so I told the headmaster that I couldn't behave in the way he had described, and would give him back the certificate of appointment.

The headmaster blinked his badger-like eyes and looked at my face. Then, eventually, he smiled and replied that he had been speaking ideally, and that since he knew very well that I wouldn't be able to live up to this, I wasn't to worry. It struck me that, if he knew as well as all that, there was no need to try and scare me in the first place.

While we were talking, the bugle sounded and pandemonium suddenly broke out in the direction of the classrooms. The headmaster said the teachers would now probably be gathered in the staff room and led the way there.

The room was a wide rectangle, and the teachers sat at desks lined up around the perimeter. When I entered, they all, as if by a prearranged signal, turned to look at me as one man. It was on the tip of my tongue to ask them who they thought they were looking at, but I went round to each and every one of them as I had been told to do and, introducing myself, presented my certificate of appointment. Most of them just rose from their seats and gave me a perfunctory bow, but the more scrupulous among them took the certificate, looked at it and passed it back again reverently. The whole thing was unreal, like one of those plays they perform at shrines. By the time I'd gone round to fifteen people and come to the sports master, I was becoming rather annoyed at going through the same performance again and again. It was all right for the others; they only had to do it once, whereas I had to keep repeating the same action. It was a pity they had no thought for other people's feelings.

One of the men I met during these preliminaries was the second master, whose name escapes me for the moment. He was apparently a Bachelor of Arts, which meant that he had graduated from a university and was, therefore, a distinguished man. He had, however, an oddly feminine voice and, what really surprised me, wore a red flannel shirt in spite of the heat. He must have been terribly hot, however thin the material was. He was as fastidious in his dress as you would expect a Bachelor of Arts to be, but his red shirt was insulting. I learned later that he wore this red shirt the whole year round because of some rare illness. He himself explained to me that he always ordered red shirts because red was good for the health. It seemed to me that his concern was needless. If what he said was true, I couldn't understand why he didn't have his coat and trousers made in red too, while he was at it.

Next I met the English master, whose name was something like Koga. He had a dreadful complexion. Most people who have sallow complexions are thin, but this fellow was sallow and fat. Years ago, when I was at primary school, there was a boy in my class, Tami Asai, whose father had the same kind of complexion. The Asais were farmers, and I asked Kiyo if all farmers had faces like that, but she said, no, Mr. Asai was sallow and fat because he was always eating unripe pumpkins. Ever since then, I have always thought that anybody with a sallow, fat face got it as a result of eating green pumpkins. There was no doubt that this English master had eaten a great many. I still haven't the faintest idea what eating unripe pumpkins has to do with being sallow and fat. I asked Kiyo once, I remember, but she just laughed and didn't answer. She probably didn't know herself.

The next man I met was the other mathematics teacher, by the name of Hotta. He was a strapping fellow, with closely cropped hair that stood up like the spines on a chestnut burr, and a face like one of those soldier-monks of the Eizan temple who were always starting revolts at the end of the Heian period. I proferred him the certificate politely, but without even looking at it he said, "So you're the new teacher. Come over to my place some time. Ha, ha, ha!"

And "ha, ha, ha" to you, I thought. You wouldn't catch me going to visit someone as ill-mannered and ignorant as him. I nicknamed him "the Porcupine" on the spot.

The teacher of Chinese classics was, as you would expect, formal, and greeted me with, "You arrived yesterday? You must be exhausted. And you start teaching tomorrow—how diligent!" He was a charming old gentleman.

The art master looked the part. The coat he wore over his kimono was of the flimsiest, transparent silk, and he flapped at himself with a fan.

"May one ask where you're from? I beg your pardon? Oh, Tokyo? Splendid! How nice to have a friend. You wouldn't think so, but I'm from Tokyo too," he simpeerd.

"Well, if you're from Tokyo, I wish I wasn't," I thought to myself.

It would take me forever to write about everyone I met, so I'd better stop here.

After the introductions had been more or less completed, the headmaster told me I could go now, but should discuss my classes with the senior mathematics master and start work in two days' time. I asked who that was and found it was none other than the Porcupine. Damn! I thought, and my heart sank. How on earth could I work under a man like him?

"Where are you staying?" he asked. "Yamashiroya? Hm. I'll be over soon to have a talk with you." With this, he picked up some chalk and walked off to the classroom. Since he was the senior teacher, his coming to my place to discuss things showed a singular lack of dignity. Still, I admired this more than making me go to see him.

I walked out of the school gate with the intention of going straight back to the inn, but since I had nothing to do there, I decided to walk around the town for a while and strolled aimlessly through the streets. I saw the prefectural government office, an old building from the last century, and the army barracks. These were no better than those of the regiment at Azabu in Tokyo. I also saw the main street, which was about half the size of Tokyo's Kagurazaka, and whose shops were poorer. This was just a small castle town which in feudal times probably only yielded its lord a paltry million and a quarter bushels of grain. I was walking along, pitying those who brag about living in a "castle town," when I suddenly found myself in front of the Yamashiroya. The town wasn't as big as it looked. I had probably already seen most of it. I went in through the gate, thinking I might as well have something to eat.

As soon as she saw me, the owner came running out

from the front office where she had been sitting. She knelt down and gave me a deep, formal bow, with her forehead touching the floor. When I had taken my shoes off and stepped up into the entrance hall, she told me that a room had just become vacant, and I was taken up to it by a maid.

The room was about fifteen feet by eighteen and was at the front of the building on the second floor. It had a large *tokonoma* recess for hanging pictures and setting flower arrangements, and was the finest room I had ever been in in all my life. Not knowing when I would get to stay in such a room again, I took off my Western clothes, put on a light summer kimono and sprawled out right in the middle of the floor to see what it felt like. It felt marvelous.

Immediately after lunch I wrote a letter to Kiyo. I hate writing letters, because my composition is poor and I have only a limited vocabulary. I had never had anyone to write to, anyway. However, I didn't want Kiyo worrying and thinking that the ship had gone down and I'd been drowned, so I made an effort and wrote her a long letter. This is what I wrote.

Dear Kiyo,

I arrived yesterday. It's a useless place. I'm sleeping in a room fifteen feet by eighteen. I gave a five-yen tip to the landlady. She got down on her knees and bowed so deeply that her forehead touched the floor. I didn't sleep well last night. I dreamed you were eating Echigo sweets, bamboo-grass wrapping and all. I'll be home next summer. I went to school today and gave all the teachers nicknames. The headmaster is the Badger, the second master is Redshirt, the English master is the Green Pumpkin, the mathematics master is the Porcupine and the art master is the Clown. I'll write and tell you more news soon.

Goodbye.

Having written the letter, I felt pleasantly drowsy, so I sprawled out in the middle of the floor again and went to sleep. This time I slept soundly, undisturbed by any dreams.

I was woken up by a loud voice saying, "This the room?"

The headmaster is the Badger, the second master is Redshirt, the English master is the Green Pumpkin, the mathematics master is the Porcupine and the art master is the Clown.

and in walked the Porcupine. To have someone start straight in with, "Sorry about this morning. Your timetable is . . ." when you have just opened your eyes is disconcerting, and it threw me completely. The classes allotted to me, however, didn't appear to present any problem, so I didn't complain. Indeed, I seemed to have got off so lightly that I wouldn't have been surprised if he'd told me I had to start first thing the next morning, instead of the day after.

When we had finished discussing classes, Hotta took in the situation and said, "You can't possibly intend to stay on here. I know a good place where you can stay. Mind you, they wouldn't normally take in anybody, but I'll put in a good word for you. You'd better move in there as soon as possible. You can see the place today, move in tomorrow, and start teaching the day after. That's the way to do it, settle everything in order."

Of course he was right. I couldn't stay in a room this size indefinitely, because even my entire salary probably wouldn't cover the cost of it. It went against the grain a little to move so soon after having laid out a five-yen tip, but if I was going to move, it would be better to do it quickly and settle somewhere. I asked Hotta to go ahead and arrange it for me. He told me to at least go and see the place with him, which I did.

The house was situated in a very quiet spot, halfway up a hillside just outside the town. The owner was a curio dealer who, judging by his nickname of Ikagin, was a charlatan. His wife was a woman about four years older than him. When I was at middle school, I learned the English word "witch," and the wife's appearance fitted exactly with my image of a witch. Still, it didn't matter to me if she was a witch; she wasn't my wife.

We eventually settled that I should move in the following day. On the way back, Hotta treated me to a dish of fruit-flavored crushed ice in a part of the town called Tōrichō.

When we had met at the school, I had thought him over-bearing and ill-mannered, but in the light of all this friendliness, he didn't seem such a bad sort after all—although, of course, he was impetuous and quick-tempered, like me. I heard later that he was the pupils' favorite teacher.

3

The day for me to start teaching came at last. The first time I entered the classroom and mounted the dais, it gave me a strange feeling. I kept thinking to myself throughout the lesson, "Am I really a teacher?"

The pupils were noisy. From time to time, one or other of them would call out, "Sir!" in an exceptionally loud voice. This began to grate on me. I'd grown used to calling teachers "sir" while I was at the School of Physics, but there is a world of difference between calling someone "sir," and being called "sir" yourself. It gave me a kind of tingling sensation down my spine.

I am neither sneaky nor a coward, but I must confess to a sad lack of audacity; and having someone call me "sir" in a loud voice gave me the same hollow feeling as hearing the midday cannon fired in the Palace grounds, on an empty stomach. I muddled through the first hour as best I could and managed to get by without being stumped by any questions. When I got back to the staff room, Hotta asked me how things had gone. I made some kind of noncommittal reply, which seemed to reassure him.

I took some chalk and left the staff room for the second class, feeling as though I were marching into enemy territory. When I reached the room, I found that the boys in this class were all bigger than those in the previous one. Since I have the typically light, compact build of a Tokyo-ite, I didn't feel that I exuded any sense of authority, even standing on the dais. I'd fight a professional wrestler if it came to it, but seeing those forty louts arrayed in front of me, I knew that I didn't have the necessary ability to dominate them with my tongue alone. But I thought that if I once showed any weakness to these oafs, I would never be able to regain control, so I began the lesson in a good loud voice and rolled my r's a bit as we do in Tokyo, to give some body to what I was saying.

At first the pupils just sat there and gaped at me in a befuddled way.

"Aha!" I thought. "Got you!" And I started using the rough, punchy language of downtown Tokyo, which is my speciality. At this, the boy right in the middle of the front row, who looked the strongest in the class, suddenly jumped to his feet and said, "Sir!"

"Here we go," I thought, but aloud I said, "Yes, what is it?"

"You're speaking too fast. I can't understand what you say. If it's all the same to you, could you speak just a bit more slower, like?"

" 'If it's all the same to you'? 'Like'? What kind of spineless language is that? If I'm speaking too quickly, I'll slow down. But I'm from Tokyo and I can't speak your dialect, so if you don't understand my accent, you'll just have to wait till you get used to it."

I carried on in this vein, and the second period went better than I had expected. Then, just as I was leaving the room, one of the boys came up to me and, showing me some impossible-looking problems, asked me, again in that dreadful dialect, to explain them. I broke out in a cold sweat. All that I could do was to tell him that I didn't understand them, but that I'd tell him next time, and beat a hasty retreat. This was the signal for general jeering, and above the overall din I could distinctly hear shouts of, "He can't do it! He can't do it!"

I went back to the staff room fuming. Damned fools! As if even a teacher could do problems like that! What was so funny about admitting it when you couldn't do something? If I'd been that good at mathematics, I wouldn't have come down here to the back of beyond for forty yen a month.

Again Hotta asked me how things had gone, and again I gave him the same noncommittal answer, but this time it didn't satisfy him, so I told him I thought all the kids in the school were blithering idiots. He gave me an odd look.

The third period, the fourth period and the hour after lunch, too, all passed in much the same fashion. I made some blunder or other in every class I took that first day. Being a teacher wasn't as easy as it looked, I realized.

All my classes for the day had finished, but I couldn't go home yet. I had to wait there by myself until three o'clock, when, apparently, the pupils had to clean up their rooms. Then I had to go and inspect those of the classes that were in my charge when they reported to me that they had finished. After that I had to check the attendance register and then, at last, I would be free. They might have bought my body with their forty-yen salary, but there was no law that said I had to be tied to the school in my free time, staring at a desk. I put up with it, however, because I thought that since everybody else was abiding by the rules without complaining it wouldn't do for me, the new boy, to make a fuss by myself.

On the way home I complained to Hotta that it was stupid to make us stay at school until after three in the afternoon, to which he replied with his usual laugh. After a while, however, he became serious and warned me not to criticize the school too much, or at least to confine my remarks to him, because there were some very strange people about. We parted at the next corner, so I didn't have a chance to hear any details.

When I arrived home, my landlord told me that he would make me a "nice cup of tea." I thought this was very kind of him, until I found out it was my tea he was going to use, and that he intended to join me in a cup. Seeing this, I thought that he was probably helping himself to a "nice cup of tea" while I was out.

He informed me that he had always been very fond of old paintings and curios, and that this had led him at last to go into business for himself. He then went on to tell me in an obsequious way that I appeared to be "a gentleman of some refinement," and wouldn't I like to begin collecting antiques as a hobby? What a ridiculous suggestion! It's true that two years before, when I had been on an errand for someone to the Imperial Hotel, they had thought I'd come to mend a lock; and that once, even, when I went to Kamakura to see the great statue of Buddha, wearing a blanket draped over my head, all the rickshaw-boys in the area had taken me for the chief coolie. In fact, I've been mistaken for something I'm not on several occasions, but *nobody* has ever suggested that I'm "a gentleman of some refinement." Generally a man's clothes and behavior speak for themselves. You only have to look at pictures to see that a man of refinement either wears a fancy hood or carries slips of paper for writing down the odes he composes. So only a rogue would call me one to my face.

I told the landlord that, not being an old man living in easy retirement, I had no use for collecting antiques as a hobby. He gave a cackling laugh at this and said that nobody liked it at first, but that once you started you just couldn't give it up. He helped himself to another cup of tea, which he drank holding the cup in a most peculiar fashion. I had, in fact, asked him to buy me some tea the previous evening, but this tasted horrible. It was too bitter and strong. One cup and you felt as though your stomach would seize up. I asked him to buy some tea that wasn't so bitter next time.

"Yes, of course, sir," he said, squeezing out the last cup in the pot for himself. It wasn't costing him anything, so he was determined to get as many cups of tea as he could. When he had gone, I prepared the next day's classes and went to bed.

Thereafter, I went to school every day, did my work, and

obeyed all the rules; and every day when I arrived home my landlord would come and offer to make me a "nice cup of tea." After about a week, I had more or less grasped the set-up at school and I understood fairly well what kind of people my landlord and his wife were. The other teachers told me that for a week to a month after receiving their certificate of appointment most people were concerned about what the boys thought of them, but this didn't worry me in the slightest. It's true that whenever I made a fool of myself in the classroom I felt bad about it at the time, but the feeling passed in half an hour or so. I'm constitutionally incapable of worrying about anything for any length of time, even if I wanted to. I was completely indifferent as to what effect my mistakes would have on the pupils, or as to how either the headmaster or second master would react to that effect. As I mentioned before, I'm not one of those people with nerves of steel, but, on the other hand, I'm very decisive. I had made up my mind that if things didn't work out for me at this school, I would go somewhere else, so I wasn't the least bit scared of either the Badger or Redshirt. Moreover, I certainly couldn't bring myself to try and charm or flatter the kids in class.

Things were all right, then, at school, but not in my lodgings. I was prepared to put up with the landlord coming and drinking my tea, providing it stopped there, but he used to bring all kinds of things with him. The first things he brought were about ten ornamental seals, which he laid out in front of me and asked me to buy. I told him that I wasn't a poor itinerant artist and didn't need them.

Following this he brought a scroll painting in which flowers and birds figured prominently and said it was by someone called Kazan, or some such name. He held it up in the *tokonoma* himself and asked me if I didn't think it was well executed. I tried not to commit myself and said that it wasn't bad, whereupon he gave me a stupid lecture, telling me that there had been two artists named Kazan—Somebody Kazan and Somebody-else Kazan—and that this picture had been painted by Somebody Kazan. Having finished his lecture he urged me to buy the picture, saying that, as it was me, I could have it for fifteen yen. I told him that I didn't have any money, but he said that I could pay anytime. He just wouldn't take no for an answer, so I told him that I wouldn't buy it even if I had the money and finally got rid of him.

Next he came in carrying a dreadful ink-stone, about the size of a ridge tile, on his shoulder. "This is Tankei stone," he said. "Tankei. From China." In fact he "Tankei-ed" me so much that I asked, half-jokingly, what Tankei was. This started him straight off on another lecture.

There are, it seems, three strata of Tankei stone, and the lower the stratum, the higher the value. All the ink-stones one saw about at that time, he said, were made from the upper stratum, but this one was definitely from the middle. "Look at the 'eyes,' sir," he continued, pointing to the natural markings on the stone. "It's unusual to find an ink-stone with three 'eyes' on it. It's wonderful for making ink on too. Just try your ink-stick on it." With this, he thrust the large stone in front of me. I asked him how much it was, and he told me that since the owner had brought it back from China and was really keen to sell it, I could have it cheap, for thirty yen. I was obviously dealing with a fool. I thought that I might be able to get by at school pretty well, but I couldn't stand this torture by antiques very much longer.

It wasn't long before the school got on my nerves too.

One evening as I was strolling through a part of the town called Ōmachi, I saw a sign next to the post office which said: *Noodles*, with the footnote, *Tokyo-style*. I've always been very fond of noodles, and when I was in Tokyo could never pass a noodle shop and smell that spicy aroma without going in. Since I had come to this town I had—what with school and antiques—forgotten about noodles; but now, seeing that sign, I just could not walk past. I thought that I would have a bowl while I was there, and went in.

The interior didn't live up to the sign outside. They had announced that this was "Tokyo-style," so the place should have been clean, but either from ignorance of Tokyo, or lack of money, it was filthy. The *tatami* matting was discolored and, for good measure, it was gritty underfoot. The walls were grimy with soot, and the ceiling, which was also black from the smoke of an oil-lamp, was so low that you involuntarily ducked your head as you walked about. The only thing that was plainly new was the sign on the wall which gave the names and prices of the various dishes. The owner had obviously bought an old building and opened it as a restaurant two or three days before. The first thing on the menu was noodles with fried prawns.

"Hey! Noodles with fried prawns," I called in a loud voice. At this, three people sitting in a corner, who had been eating noodles with a hissing, sucking sound, all looked across at me together. The inside of the shop was dark and I hadn't noticed them before, but I now recognized them as pupils at the school. We said good evening to each other and I got on with my meal. I hadn't had noodles for a long time and they tasted good, so I polished off four bowls.

The next day I walked blithely into the classroom, only to be confronted with the words A FRIED PRAWN FOR THE TEACHER, written in enormous letters, covering the blackboard. When they saw the look on my face, everyone burst out laughing. This struck me as absurd, and I asked them what was so funny about fried prawns, to which one of the pupils replied, "But four bowls! That's a bit much, like." I told them that it was my money and that it had nothing to do with them whether I ate four bowls or five. I then went through the lesson as quickly as I could and returned to the staff room.

Ten minutes later I walked into the next class and

there on the board was 4 (FOUR) BOWLS OF FRIED PRAWNS! LAUGHING STRICTLY PROHIBITED.

When I'd read what they'd written on the blackboard in the last class I hadn't been particularly worried, but this time I was really annoyed. A joke's a joke, but when you take it too far it becomes mischief.

Proportion is the rule in all things. If a joke goes to malicious bounds, or if, for example, admiration turns to jealousy, nobody çan stomach them. These things are like rice-cake, which is delicious toasted but horrible if it's burned black. Country people don't have the ability to make this kind of fine distinction and have no idea where to draw the line.

These kids had been brought up in a castle town that was so small that you could see all its sights in an hour, and having no other accomplishments to pride themselves on, were as excited about this fried-prawn incident as if it had been the Russo-Japanese war. Poor devils! Their whole education had been such that they were as warped and stunted as a maple tree grown in a flowerpot. I wouldn't have minded if their humor had been innocent. I would have laughed with them. But, for young boys, they were strangely spiteful.

I cleaned the blackboard without a word, then turned to them and said, "Do you think it's funny to play tricks like that? It's a lily-livered kind of joke! Do you know what lily-livered means?" One of them answered, "Yeah, it means getting angry when you're laughed at for something you've done, like." Oafs! I could have wept to think that I'd come all the way from Tokyo to teach this crowd. I told them that they weren't going to have the last word with me, so they'd better shut up and get on with their work. Then I began the lesson.

In the next class I was greeted by the following words on the blackboard: IF YOU EAT FRIED PRAWNS YOU HAVE TO HAVE THE LAST WORD. It was all beyond

Ten minutes later I walked into the next class and there on the board was *4 (FOUR) BOWLS OF FRIED PRAWNS! LAUGHING STRICTLY PROHIBITED.*

me. I just didn't know what to do with them. Telling them that I had no intention of teaching such impertinent brats, I walked straight out of the room. If this was how things were going to be I preferred antiques to school.

I found, however, that I'd cooled down considerably after going home and sleeping on the fried-prawn affair. I went to school the following day and everybody was present. I couldn't make out what it all meant.

The next three days passed without incident, but on the evening of the fourth day I went to a place called Sumida, and while I wàs there had some rice dumplings. Sumida was a hot-spring resort about ten minutes by train, or thirty minutes on foot, from the town, and besides restaurants, hotels and a park, it boasted a brothel quarter. I had heard that the food there was very good, so I dropped in to try it on my way back from the hot-spring bath. This time I met none of the boys from school and thought that nobody would know.

I went to school the next day and once again walked blithely into the classroom for the first period. There on the board was TWO PLATES OF DUMPLINGS—7 SEN. It was quite true: I had eaten two plates of dumplings, and I had paid seven sen. What a confounded nuisance those kids were!

I went into the second period, convinced that there would be something written on the blackboard, and sure enough there was: THE DUMPLINGS IN THE BROTHEL QUARTER ARE SIMPLY DELICIOUS. I was dumbfounded.

No sooner had the incident of the dumplings passed than a red towel became the topic of conversation. I didn't understand what they were on about until I found out that it was connected with a habit of mine. Ever since I had arrived in the town I had made it a practice to go to Sumida each day for a hot-spring bath. Nothing else in the area was a patch on Tokyo, but the hot springs were marvelous.

Thinking that since I was there I might as well take advantage of them and take a bath every day, I used to go over there in the evening for the exercise. Unfortunately, I always had a large Western bath-towel dangling from my hand. Not only had the spring water discolored this towel, but the red stripes in it had run, so that when you caught just a glimpse of it, it looked scarlet. I had that towel dangling from my hand every single day, both going and coming, whether on the train or walking. That's how the pupils came to call me Red-towel. What a harassing thing it was to live in a small town!

There's more.

The hot-spring bath was housed in a new three-story building. If you went first class, for only eight sen they lent you a bathrobe, an attendant washed you, and a girl served you tea in one of those elegant, shallow cups that they use in the tea ceremony. I always went first class, and the boys at school began to say that it was extravagant to go first class on forty yen a month.

There's still more.

The bath itself was about fifteen feet by eighteen and was lined with granite. You generally found about thirteen or fourteen people soaking in it, but sometimes it was empty. The water was about breast-high and I used to swim in the bath for exercise. When I was sure nobody was about, I would amuse myself by swimming around the perimeter of the tank. However, one day I came down from the third floor in high spirits, wondering whether I would be able to have a swim, and glancing at the partition running along the front of the bath I found a large notice in bold, black letters which warned, *No Swimming in the Bath*. There could scarcely have been many people who swam in the bath, so the notice had probably been especially written for me. I gave up swimming after that, but I was taken aback to find written on the blackboard when I went to school: NO SWIMMING IN THE BATH.

The thought that the whole school was ganging up to spy on me was depressing. The pupils didn't say anything to me directly, but I began to wonder why I had ever come to this poky little town. Not only did I have to put up with this kind of thing at school, I also had to continue enduring torture by antiques when I got home.

Everybody on the staff had to take it in turns to do night duty; everybody, that is, except the Badger and Redshirt. When I asked how they managed to get out of this I was told that the positions of headmaster and second master at middle schools were by Imperial approval and carried the rank of *sōnin*, and that they were, therefore, exempted. What a load of rubbish! Why should they draw fat salaries, work short hours, and then be excused from night duty? It was unfair. They made up rules to suit their own purposes and had the gall to behave as if this were the most natural thing in the world. I grumbled a lot about it, but Hotta said that one person on his own couldn't achieve anything, however much reason for complaint he had. I couldn't see what numbers had to do with it; one person or two, if a complaint was justified, it was justified. When I said this to Hotta, he quoted the English words, "Might is right." I was unable to grasp the meaning of this, so he explained that it meant that the strong got the privileges. That much I'd known for a long time and I didn't need it spelled out for me now; but that was one thing and night duty was another. Besides which, nobody could possibly agree that the Badger and Redshirt came into the category of "the strong." Anyway, arguments notwithstanding, it eventually came round to my turn for night duty.

My restless and nervous disposition has always made it impossible for me to get a sound sleep unless I'm in my own bed, with my own bedding. Because of this I scarcely ever went to spend the night at a friend's house when I was a boy. It stands to reason, then, that if I didn't even like sleeping at a friend's, I was going to hate sleeping in a school dormitory. But if this was included in the forty yen, I would just have to put up with it.

The teachers and day-boys had all gone home and it was very dull being left there by myself with nothing to do. The room that the teacher on night duty used was at the west end of the dormitories, which were at the rear of the classrooms. I went to take a look, but the room was catching the full force of the afternoon sun and was too hot to stay in. Like everything else in the country, the heat too was slow and deliberate. It would still be hot in autumn.

I had the food for the boarders and myself brought in and got the evening meal over quickly, but I was staggered how horrible it was. I didn't see how the boys had the energy to behave in the rowdy way they did on this food. The way they put that food away in no time at half past four in the afternoon was nothing short of heroic.

The meal was over, but I could hardly go to bed yet because it was still broad daylight. I fancied going to the hot spring, but I wasn't sure whether it was right or not to go out when you were on night duty. I couldn't bear, however, to just sit there gazing miserably into space like a convict doing a term of penal servitude. When I had first come to the school and asked the caretaker for the teacher on night duty, he'd told me that he was out. I had thought it peculiar at the time, but now that it was my turn I began to understand why and decided that I would be right to go out. When I told the caretaker I would be back shortly, he asked me if I had some business to attend to. I told him no, it wasn't business, I was just going to the hot spring for a bath, and left. It was a pity I hadn't brought my red towel with me from my lodgings, but I could borrow one at the bathhouse.

I had a leisurely bath at the hot spring, getting in and out of the tank several times. When, at last, evening came, I took the train back to Komachi station. This was only about a quarter of a mile from the school, so I decided to walk. I hadn't gone more than a few yards, when I saw the Badger coming from the other direction. He was probably planning to go to the hot spring himself. Although he was hurrying along, he caught sight of my face as he passed, so I nodded a greeting. He stopped and said in a serious tone, "Correct me if I'm wrong, but aren't you supposed to be on night duty?" I found this "correct me if I'm wrong" irritating, because it had only been two hours ago that he'd said, "Ah yes, you're on duty tonight, aren't you?" and thanked me in advance. Headmasters always have to make a tortuous detour to say what they mean. I was angry, so, as a parting shot, I said, "Yes, I'm on night duty. Which is exactly why I'm going back to spend the night at school now." With that, I walked off with an unconcerned look on my face.

I had gone as far as the crossroads at Tatemachi, when this time I ran into Hotta. This was such a small town that you couldn't put one foot outside the door without meeting somebody you knew.

"Hey! Aren't you on night duty?" he asked.

"Yes, that's right."

"You can't just go walking off like this, you know. It's outrageous."

I told him in a rather haughty fashion that I didn't find it outrageous in the slightest, and that, on the contrary, it would have been outrageous to have stayed in. He then—and this sounded very unlike Hotta—complained about my negligence and said that I'd be in trouble if I ran into the headmaster or Redshirt. I retorted that, as a matter of fact, I'd just met the headmaster, and he'd said that I was quite right to come out for a walk when it was as hot as this, because it was the only way to make night duty bearable. By now I was tired of the whole thing, so I left Hotta standing there and went back to school.

Darkness fell soon afterwards and I called the caretaker

to my room for a chat. After about two hours, however, I grew tired of this and decided to go to bed, even though I didn't expect to sleep yet. I changed into a thin night kimono, lifted the side of the mosquito net, pulled back the red blanket and, flinging my backside down onto the mattress with a thump, lay on my back. It's been a habit of mine to flop down onto the mattress when I go to bed ever since I was a child.

I remember once when I was in lodgings in Ogawamachi a law student who lived downstairs came and complained to me about this bad habit of mine. All law students are feeble, but they have the gift of the gab. This one was no exception. He went on and on talking a lot of tedious nonsense, but I shut him up. I told him that if the building shook when I went to bed it wasn't my backside's fault, it was the building's; so if he had anything to say he should not come to me, but go and tell the landlord.

Since the room I was in now wasn't upstairs, it didn't matter how much noise I made when I fell onto the mattress. I have to throw myself down onto the bed with as much force as I can, because I just don't feel rested otherwise.

I was lying there, stretching my legs right out and thinking how pleasant it was, when I felt something hop onto each leg. Whatever they were felt rough, which meant they weren't fleas. I jumped and kicked my legs about two or three times under the blanket, whereupon the number of scratchy things increased. I could feel them in five or six places on my shins, two or three were on my thighs, one got squashed under my backside, and one even hopped to my navel. This really gave me a fright and I leaped up and flung off the blanket. About fifty or sixty grasshoppers jumped out of the bed. It had given me an eerie sensation to feel them on me when I hadn't known what they were, but now that they had emerged in their true colors and I could see that they were only grasshoppers, my feeling changed to anger. "All right, you scurvy little pests," I thought. "Frighten me, will you? I'll show you!" I snatched up the pillow and hit out at them two or three times, but they were so small that the more force I hit them with, the less effect it had. I was doing no good at all this way, so I sat down on the bed again and, using the pillow as women do a rolled-up mat to beat the *tatami* when they're cleaning, I laid about me. Not only were the grasshoppers thrown into a panic, they were also thrown up into the air by the force of the pillow. They landed on my shoulders, head and face, and bumped against me. Since I could scarcely hit those that were on my face with the pillow, I grabbed them in my hand and hurled them away from me as hard as I could. This had no effect, however, for no matter how hard I flung them, they hit the mosquito net and just stayed there where they had been thrown, gripping the net and wafting gently backwards and forwards. They didn't die, they didn't do anything. At the end of about half an hour I had at last managed to exterminate them. I then took a broom and swept out the corpses.

The caretaker came and asked me what was the matter.

"What do you mean, 'what's the matter'?" I shouted. "Have you ever heard of anyone keeping grasshoppers in his bed? Idiot!" He said he didn't know anything about it, but I thought this was a poor excuse, so I threw the broom out onto the verandah. The caretaker picked it up timidly and slunk off.

I lost no time in calling for three of the boarders to represent the dormitories. Six, in fact, arrived. Six or ten, it was all the same to me. I stood there in my night ki-mono, with the sleeves pulled back to the shoulders ready for action, and began the parley.

"What did you put grasshoppers in my bed for?"

"Er, what's a grasshopper?" asked the boy nearest me. His self-possession bordered on insolence. It looked as though it wasn't only the headmaster at this school who

*"All right, you scurvy little pests," I thought. "Frighten me, will you?
I'll show you!"*

could juggle with words: the pupils were going to do it too.

"You don't know what a grasshopper is? All right. I'll show you," I said. But I'd swept every last one of them out, so I couldn't. I called the caretaker again and told him to bring the grasshoppers back. He replied that he'd already thrown them on the rubbish heap and should he go and get them again? I told him yes, he should, and he scuttled off. He reappeared at last with about ten of the dead grasshoppers on a piece of notepaper and said that he was terribly sorry, but it was so dark that unfortunately these were all he could find, and he would find some more for me tomorrow. Even the caretaker was a fool.

I showed one of the insects to the boys and said, "*This* is a grasshopper. Look at the size of you and you still don't know what a grasshopper is."

The boy on the far left of the group had the cheek to try and score off me by saying, "That's not a grasshopper. It's a locust, like."

"You damned idiot! A grasshopper and a locust are the same thing. And while we're about it, stop finishing every confounded sentence with 'like.' It sounds like 'tyke,' and if that's what you're trying to call me come straight out with it and don't mumble." I thought that would shut him up, but no.

"Like and tyke are different, like," he said.

Like, like, like! That's all you ever heard out of them.

"Anyway," I went on, "grasshoppers or locusts, why did you put them in my bed? Did I ask you to?"

"Nobody put them there."

"How else could they have got into my bed if nobody put them there?"

"Locusts like warm places. They probably crawled in by themselves."

"Don't talk rubbish! Grasshoppers don't just waltz their way into beds by themselves. And if you think I'm going

53

to put up with people waltzing them in, you're mistaken. Now, come on. Speak out."

"It's all very well to say 'speak out,' but we can't explain something we didn't do."

What a miserable lot they were! If they hadn't the nerve to own up to what they'd done, they shouldn't have done it. As long as I couldn't offer any proof, they intended to put on a wooden face and deny all knowledge of the affair.

I got up to a few pranks myself when I was at middle school, but when a teacher asked who was responsible I owned up like a man every single time. If you've done something, you've done it; and if you haven't, you haven't. It's as simple as that. I may have played tricks when I was at school, but at least I was always honest about it. If I'd intended to lie in order to escape the consequences of what I'd done, I wouldn't have done it in the first place. Mischief and punishment are inseparable. It's the thought of punishment that adds spice to getting into mischief. I know of no society that tolerates people so despicable that they expect to have their fun without paying for it. It was obvious that these kids, when they left school, were going to turn into the kind of people who borrow money and refuse to pay it back. They come to school, tell lies, cheat and skulk about in the shadows, play malicious tricks on people, and then when they graduate they strut about, laboring under the misapprehension that they have received an education. They were the scum of the earth!

It made me sick to talk to people with such putrid ideas, so I excused the six of them, telling them that if they didn't want to own up they didn't have to, but that I felt sorry for anyone going to middle school who didn't have the ability to distinguish between what was decent and what wasn't. My appearance and behavior may not be very refined and I may not speak elegantly, but I was convinced that, at heart, I was a lot better person than they were.

They all strolled away calmly, looking far superior to me

because I was a teacher in name only, without any of the qualities usually associated with that profession. Nevertheless, their very composure was an indication of what kind of people they were. I would never have had the nerve to behave like that under such circumstances.

I got back into bed again and lay down, but the inside of the net was filled with the buzzing of mosquitoes. They must have got in during the fracas a little while ago. It was too much trouble to burn every one of them individually with a candle, so I took down the net, laid it out in several long folds, and began to give it a good shaking inside the room. I shook it lengthwise and breadthwise and put so much energy into it that one of the cords with a metal ring attached to it, used for hanging up the net, came flying over and cracked me on the back of my hand hard enough to make a saint swear.

I was a little calmer when I got into bed for the third time, but I just couldn't sleep. I looked at my watch and found it was half past ten. When you came to think about it, I'd really picked a great place to live in. I felt very sorry for middle-school teachers if these were the kind of kids they had to teach all the time. It was a wonder they didn't run out of teachers. You had to be extremely patient and even a bit dense, perhaps, to take on a job like this. It was definitely not for me.

This train of thought led me to Kiyo. What an admirable person she was. She was only an old woman, without education or social position, but she had a noble character. I had never before felt particularly grateful for all she had done for me, but now, miles away from home and all by myself, I appreciated her kindness for the first time. If she wanted to eat sweets from Echigo, then I ought to go there and get some for her. She was worth it. Kiyo had always praised me and said that I was unselfish and straightforward, but she was a far finer person than me. How I wished I could have been with her then.

I was stretching myself and thinking about Kiyo when suddenly overhead I heard what must have been thirty or forty boys all stamping on the floor in time. The drumming was so great that I was afraid the ceiling was going to cave in on me. Not only were they stamping, they were letting out loud war whoops of proportionate volume. I was afraid something serious had happened and shot out of bed. But no sooner was I up than it dawned on me that it was the pupils getting their own back for what I'd said to them earlier.

"You know what you did was wrong," I thought. "And what you did stands until you apologize. If you had any sense of what's right you'd go to bed, feel sorry for what you've done, and come and apologize in the morning. The least you can do is be ashamed of yourselves and go to sleep quietly.

"This dormitory wasn't put up as a pig-pen. Stop behaving like raving lunatics! Right! I'll show you!"

All these thoughts raced through my head as, still dressed for bed, I cleared the stairs up to the second floor in three and a half bounds. But, oddly enough, the racket I had heard going on upstairs had stopped. Everything was quiet. There wasn't even the sound of voices, much less footsteps. Strange.

The lamps had already been turned out, so I wouldn't have been able to see anybody clearly, but I would have been able to sense if they were anywhere. There wasn't so much as a mouse hiding in the corridor which ran the length of the building from east to west. The moon shone in at the far end of the corridor, making an area as bright as day. It was all very peculiar.

I've always dreamed a lot ever since I was a child. I was often laughed at for suddenly sitting up in bed and babbling something in my sleep. Once, I remember, when I was about sixteen or seventeen, I dreamed I found a diamond. Then, sitting bolt upright, I started vehemently asking my brother, who was sleeping beside me, what he'd done with it. I was the laughing-stock of the family for three days and felt very embarrassed about the whole thing. In view of all this, it was possible that I'd dreamed everything up till now. I was positive, however, that the pupils had been making a noise.

I was standing in the middle of the corridor, mulling these things over in my mind, when suddenly from the end which was bathed in moonlight there came, "One, two, three . . ." And then, "Yahoooo!" from about thirty or forty throats. This was immediately followed by the same drumming sound as before, as they all stamped in time on the floorboards. So I *had* been right. It hadn't been a dream.

"Be quiet!" I shouted in a voice as loud as any of theirs. "It's the middle of the night!" And I started to dash down the corridor.

The part I was running along was dark and the only thing I had to guide me was the moonlit patch at the far end. I can only have run about five or six yards when, right in the middle of the corridor, something large and hard hit me across the shin. I let out a yell of pain, which was still ringing in my ears as I went sprawling headlong onto my face. I cursed and got to my feet, but I couldn't run. However impatient I was to go on, I just couldn't control my leg. This irritated me so much that I hopped the rest of the way on my good leg. But when I came to the place where the noise had been there wasn't a footstep or a voice to be heard. Everything was as quiet as the grave. I knew all men had an element of cowardice in them, but theirs went to ridiculous lengths. These weren't human beings, they were pigs.

I was now determined that I wasn't going to leave until I had dragged them out of their hiding places and made them apologize. With this in mind, I tried to open one of the dormitory doors to look inside, but I couldn't. I don't know whether it was locked or whether they'd set a desk or something up against it, but, however much I pushed, it wouldn't budge. I tried the dormitory opposite, on the north side of the corridor, but with the same result. While I was fuming and trying to get the door open to haul the kids out, another war whoop and more stamping of feet started up at the eastern end of the passage. "Oh, so it's a conspiracy, is it?" I thought. "The kids at the eastern end and the western end have got together to make a fool of me." This much I realized, but I didn't know what to do about it. To tell the truth, I have more courage than wisdom. I never know what to do at times like that.

I had, however, no intention of being beaten. If I left things as they were I would lose a great deal of face. I couldn't have it said that a Tokyoite lacked spirit. I would never live it down if it were known that I'd been made fun of by a bunch of snotty-nosed kids and cried myself to sleep because I didn't know what to do about it. My ancestors were bodyguards to the Shōgun, the military ruler of Japan in feudal times. The Shōgun's personal retainers all belonged to the ancient Minamoto family, who came down in direct line from the Emperor Seiwa. That is to say, one of my ancestors was that great knight, Tada Mitsunaka. I was, therefore, of much higher birth than that crowd of peasants. I must admit, however, that I regretted not having a better head on my shoulders. I was in a spot, not knowing what to do, but even so I was not going to be beaten. The reason I didn't know what to do was that I am so honest. But think about it. If an honest man can't win in this world, who can?

I was determined that if I didn't win tonight, I would tomorrow; and if I didn't win tomorrow, I would the day after; and if not then, I would have food sent in to me and wait there until I did win. Having decided this, I squatted cross-legged in the middle of the corridor and waited for the dawn. The mosquitoes kept buzzing around me, but I didn't care. I ran my hand along the shin I had hurt earlier and found it was slippery. It was probably bleeding. Let it bleed! It wasn't long before the weariness from my recent exertion made itself felt and, without meaning to, I dropped off to sleep.

I was woken up by some kind of excitement nearby. "Damn!" I thought, and sat up quickly. The door to the right of where I was sitting was partly open and two of the pupils stood in front of me. As soon as I had gathered my wits I grabbed the leg of the boy who was standing right in front of me and yanked it for all I was worth. The boy crashed down onto his back. Take that! The other boy looked a little confused, so I took advantage of this and, springing at him, caught him by the shoulders and gave him a good shaking. He was stupified and could only blink at me. "Right! Come down to my room," I said. They both followed as meekly as lambs. It had been light for quite a while.

Back in my room, I demanded an explanation from the boys, but pigs are pigs, whether you beat them, thrash them or whatever you do, so to all my questions they just said they didn't know anything. They had no intention of confessing. "I don't know" seemed to be all they were prepared to say on the subject. Gradually one, then another of the pupils came down from upstairs, until finally they were all gathered in my room. They looked sleepy and their eyelids were puffy. Weak-kneed brats! A man ought to look in better condition than that after only missing one night's sleep. I told them to go and wash their faces and then come back and argue, but nobody made a move.

I had been wrangling with over fifty of them for about an hour, when the Badger unexpectedly appeared. I heard later that the caretaker had gone to get him, saying that there was a big disturbance at the school. It was precisely because he was the kind of man who had no more pride than to go and call the headmaster for such a paltry reason that he was a caretaker in a middle school.

The headmaster listened both to my account of the affair and also to a few of the boys' excuses. He told them that he would deal with them later, but in the meantime to attend school as usual. He added that if they didn't hurry up and wash and have their breakfast they'd be late for school. And, with that, he dismissed them all. What laxity! If it had been me I'd have expelled all the boarders on the spot. It was because of this lethargic attitude of his that the pupils made a fool of the teacher on night duty.

The headmaster then turned to me and said, "You must be tired out after all that worry. Why don't you take the day off today?"

"No, thank you," I replied. "I wasn't in the least worried. As long as there's breath in my body I wouldn't worry if that kind of thing happened every night. Furthermore, if I were too tired to teach because I'd missed a night's sleep I'd return one day's money out of my salary."

I don't know what the headmaster thought of this, but, after staring at my face for a while, he said, "But your face is all swollen, you know."

My face did, in fact, feel rather heavy and it itched all over. I must have been badly bitten by mosquitoes. Scratching my face violently, I replied that however swollen my face was, my mouth was still in working order, so it wouldn't stop me from giving lessons. At this the headmaster complimented me on my energy. Actually, I don't think it was a compliment. I think he was making fun of me.

5

"Would you like to come fishing?" asked Redshirt. He was so soft-spoken that it made me feel quite uneasy to hear him. You couldn't have told from his voice whether he was a man or a woman. A man ought to speak like one, especially if he's a university graduate. If I, who had only been to the School of Physics, could speak as I did, it was positively indecent for a Bachelor of Arts to have such an effeminate voice.

I made some reply that wasn't calculated to sound enthusiastic, at which Redshirt had the cheek to ask me if I'd ever been fishing. As a matter of fact, I hadn't very often. But once when I was a boy I caught three silver carp in the fishing-pond at Koume in Tokyo. On another occasion— it was at a fair held in front of the Bishamon shrine in the Zenkokuji temple in Kagurazaka —I managed to hook a carp about eight inches long, but just when I thought I had it, it fell back into the water with a splash. I still have a sense of disappointment when I think about it, even now. I told Redshirt about this, but he just thrust his chin forward and gave his simpering laugh. I wished he wouldn't laugh in that affected way.

"Well then," he continued, "you don't really know about the joys of fishing yet, do you? I'll teach you, if you like." He seemed highly delighted, but I had no desire whatsoever to be taught. People who fish or hunt are all cruel. If they weren't, they couldn't enjoy taking life. It stands to reason that even fish and birds prefer being alive to being dead. It's different if you have to fish or hunt in order to live, but it seems like gross overindulgence to me

61

that a man living a perfectly comfortable life has to kill living things to get a good night's sleep. This was what I thought, but I saw no hope of winning an argument with a Bachelor of Arts—they're all glib—and I kept quiet about it. Seeing this, Redshirt thought I'd given in and, pressing the point, said, "I'll teach you immediately. Are you free today? Why don't you come with us? I was going with Yoshikawa, but it will be more company with three of us. Do come."

Yoshikawa was the art master, the one I'd nicknamed the Clown. I don't know what his idea was, but he was in and out of Redshirt's house every morning and evening and danced attendance on him everywhere he went. They were supposed to be colleagues—equals—but looking at them you'd have thought they were master and man. It didn't surprise me that the Clown was going fishing with Redshirt, because he always went everywhere with him. What I did wonder, however, was why they'd invited someone as unsociable as me to join them when they could have gone by themselves. Probably so they could lord it over me and show off what fine anglers they were. Well, I'm not one to be impressed by that sort of thing; nor do I stand and gape just because someone manages to catch two or three tunnies. I may not have been very good, but, not being subhuman, I thought I would probably hook something. Anyway, if I refused, Redshirt, being the kind of man he was, would undoubtedly jump to the wrong conclusion and think I'd refused because I was no good at fishing, and not because I disliked it. So I agreed.

After school I called in at my lodgings, got ready, and went to meet the other two at the station. Then we all went down to the beach together. There was only one boatman, and the boat itself was long and narrow, like nothing I had ever seen when I lived in Tokyo.

I'd been looking over the boat, but could see no sign of any fishing rods. I wondered how you could fish without a rod and asked the Clown what he intended to do. He stroked his chin and replied in a professional manner that when you fished out to sea you didn't use a rod, and that, "actually," you only needed a line. I felt very humiliated and wished I'd kept my mouth shut.

The boatman rowed out to sea with slow, leisurely strokes, but experience will tell, and when I looked back, I found that we were already so far out that the beach looked very small in the distance. The pagoda of the Kōhakuji temple tapered needlelike above the trees and, a way off, Aojima Island floated on the water. Nobody lived on this island, and looking closely I could see why. It was just a conglomeration of rocks and pine trees. Redshirt remarked how exquisite the scenery was, and Yoshikawa, the Clown, lisped his agreement. I didn't know whether it was exquisite or not, but it certainly gave me a pleasant feeling to look at it. It felt good to be there on that vast expanse of water, being fanned by a sea breeze. I was starving.

"Look at that pine tree," Redshirt said to Yoshikawa. "The trunk is perfectly straight and the top of the tree spreads out like an umbrella. It might have been painted by Turner."

The Clown replied that it was "straight out of a Turner," and that the curve was perfect. I didn't have any idea what "Turner" meant, but thinking that I could get along very well without the knowledge, I kept quiet.

The boat skirted around to the right of the island. There were no waves at all. It was so calm, in fact, that it was difficult to realize you were on the sea. I was having a very pleasant time, thanks to Redshirt. If possible, I would have liked to land on the island and see what it was like, so pointing out a rock, I asked if the boat couldn't pull in there. I was told by Redshirt that it could be done, but that the fishing wasn't any good too close to land. Yoshikawa then, adressing himself to Redshirt, came up with the uncalled-for suggestion that we call the place Turner Island. Redshirt thought this was a good idea and said that that was what we would always call it from then on. I hoped that I hadn't been included in that "we." Aojima Island was fine as far as I was concerned.

"Imagine Raphael's Madonna standing on that rock," said Yoshikawa. "It would make a superb picture. Don't you agree?"

"Let's not talk about Madonnas," replied Redshirt, and gave his disconcertingly effeminate laugh. Yoshikawa, with a glance at me, said it was all right, because there was nobody to hear. He then deliberately turned away with a smirk. This made me feel uncomfortable. Madonna or belladonna, it was all the same to me. He could put what he liked up on the rock. But saying things that other people don't understand and, moreover, not caring whether they hear *because* they don't understand, is boorish. In spite of his behavior, Yoshikawa still had the gall to say that he was a Tokyoite. Madonna was probably the nickname of Redshirt's favorite geisha. Well, if he wanted to stand a geisha under a pine tree on an uninhabited island, let him. And the Clown could paint her in oils and show the picture in an exhibition.

The boatman dropped anchor, saying that this was probably a good place to fish. In reply to Redshirt's question as to how deep the water was, the boatman said that it was six fathoms. Redshirt cast his line and remarked that there wasn't much likelihood of finding bream at that depth. So our intrepid second master thought he was going to catch himself a lordly bream, did he? He didn't have a hope! But Yoshikawa, always the flatterer, said that with Redshirt's skill and the sea being so calm, he was bound to get a bite. Then he too threw his line over the side and paid it out.

The lines had a lead weight at the end, but no float. It seemed to me that fishing without a float was like trying to

64

"Let's not talk about Madonnas," replied Redshirt, and gave his disconcertingly effeminate laugh. Yoshikawa, with a glance at me, said it was all right, because there was nobody to hear.

take one's temperature without a thermometer. I was thinking that I couldn't possibly do it, when Redshirt turned to me and said, "Come on. You try, too. Do you have any line?" When I told him that I had more than enough line but no float, he answered that only amateurs needed a float. "When the line touches the bottom like this," he said, "you use your index finger to take its pulse, as it were, where it passes over the side of the boat. Then, when you get a bite, you can feel it. —There! I've got one." He suddenly started to pull in his line. But when it was in, there was nothing on the hook. All that had happened was that the bait had gone. Good!

"Oh, what a pity!" said Yoshikawa. "I'm sure it was a big one. If it got away from you, my dear sir, with all your skill, we'll have to be exceptionally careful today. Still, even if it did get away, it's better to fish your way than to sit staring at a float all day long. Not being able to fish without a float is like not being able to ride a bicycle without brakes."

The way the Clown was prattling on made me want to give him a good hiding more than ever. Since I also belong to the human race, and Redshirt hadn't rented the entire ocean, I felt that at least one bonito would feel duty-bound to come and give me a bite. I threw the weight over the side with a splash and manipulated the line with the tips of my fingers as the mood took me.

Not long after, I felt something jerking at the line. I thought about it. It had to be a fish. The line wouldn't be twitching if what I'd caught hadn't been alive. "Done it!" I thought. "I've caught a fish." I yanked the line in hand over hand.

"I say, you've caught one," said Yoshikawa. "Ah, the power of youth is a frightening thing."

While he was being sarcastic I had almost pulled the line in, and only about five feet of it remained submerged in the water. I looked over the side and saw that there was a striped fish, like a goldfish in shape, on the end of the line. It was drifting to and fro in the water, and as I pulled in the line it came floating to the top. Hurray! As the fish broke water it started to wriggle and splash and I got a faceful of salt water. I managed to grab it at last, but I couldn't get the hook out of its mouth. The hand I was holding the fish with became horribly slimy. I found the whole thing too much trouble, so I swung the line and threw the fish into the small fish well in the middle of the boat. It soon died.

Redshirt and the Clown looked on in surprise. I swished my hands about in the sea to wash them, but when I held them up to my nose they still smelled fishy. I'd had enough. I didn't want to take hold of a fish, whatever I caught, and I don't suppose the fish wanted to be taken hold of either. I quickly rolled up my line.

"Well, first blood to you. Congratulations," Yoshikawa said. And then he added with his customary cheek, "But only a *goruki* . . ."

"Yes," Redshirt broke in, trying to be funny, "it sounds like that Russian writer Gorki."

"You're absolutely right," agreed Yoshikawa immediately. "It's exactly like the Russian author."

So what? Gorki's a Russian writer, Maruki's[1] a photographer at Shiba, and if people were honest you wouldn't need *any* kind of "key." Dropping foreigners' names one after the other in a conversation was a bad habit of Redshirt's. It made it sound as though he were speaking in italics. Everyone has his own speciality, and being a teacher of mathematics, I hadn't the faintest idea what the difference between Gorki and Turkey was. He should have made allowances for that. If he had to use foreign words, why didn't he talk about Benjamin Franklin's autobiography? Or mention "pushing to the front" —the phrase they used to use to explain the art of capitalistic living? These were things even I knew about, things that were often mentioned in middle-school textbooks. Redshirt used sometimes to bring a bright red magazine called *Imperial Literature* to school and read it avidly. Hotta once told me that all the foreign names came from this magazine. *Imperial Literature* had a lot to answer for.

Redshirt and Yoshikawa continued to fish for all they were worth and after an hour had caught about fifteen or sixteen fish between them. Strangely enough, every time they pulled a fish in it turned out to be a *goruki*. They couldn't catch a bream for love or money. Redshirt remarked to the Clown that there seemed to be a predominance of Russian literature that day. To which Yoshikawa replied that if Redshirt could only catch *goruki*, he couldn't expect anything better. I asked the boatman if these small *goruki* were any good to eat, but he said no, they were full of bones and tasted awful. The only thing they were good for, apparently, was fertilizer. Redshirt and the Clown were frantically trying to catch fertilizer. I felt very sorry for them. One fish had been enough for me, so I had lain down in the middle of the boat and looked up at the broad expanse of the sky. It was a far more elegant way of spending the time than fishing.

While I was lying there I heard the other two begin to whisper together. I couldn't make out what they were saying very well, and I didn't want to. As I looked up at the sky I was thinking of Kiyo. I knew how much pleasure it would have given her if I'd had the money and could have brought her down to a beautiful place like this for a holiday. Being with Yoshikawa even spoiled scenery as beautiful as this. Kiyo was just a wrinkled old woman, but I wouldn't have been ashamed to take her anywhere. A person like Yoshikawa, on the other hand, was someone you'd want to stay clear of whether he was in a carriage, on a boat, or at the top of the Ryōunkaku tower in Asakusa. I was sure that if I'd been the second master and Redshirt had been me, the Clown would have been fickle enough and impudent enough to flatter me and jeer at Redshirt. They say people from Tokyo are insincere, and I could see why. With a person like Yoshikawa going around the countryside telling everyone that he was from Tokyo, it was no wonder that country people thought the word Tokyoite synonymous with insincerity.

As these thoughts were going through my mind, I became aware that the two of them were tittering. They were saying something between giggles, but it only came in snatches and I couldn't get the gist of it.

"What? Not really! . . ."

". . . No, it's perfectly true . . . doesn't know, so . . . It's a shame."

"Never! . . ."

"Put grasshoppers . . . I mean it."

I hadn't really been listening up till then, but when I heard Yoshikawa say "grasshoppers," I suddenly pricked up my ears. For some reason he'd emphasized that word so that I heard it clearly and had deliberately slurred what came after. I continued to listen without moving.

"That Hotta again? . . ."

"Yes, possibly . . ."

"Fried prawns . . . Ha, ha, ha, ha, ha!"

"Stirred up . . ."

"Dumplings too?"

I had only caught fragments of the conversation, but it was obvious from such words as "grasshoppers," "fried prawns" and "dumplings" that I was the subject of their private talk. If they wanted to talk why didn't they speak up? If what they were saying was confidential they shouldn't have invited me. The pair of them made me sick. Grasshoppers or clodhoppers, I wasn't the one to blame. The headmaster had asked me to leave things to him for the time being, and out of deference to his position I was holding my peace at the moment. Yoshikawa, who was no better than a court jester, had a nerve, giving criticism

69

where it wasn't wanted. He should have sat in the corner and sucked his paintbrush. I wasn't worried about the grasshopper business because I would get around to settling it by myself all in good time, but I must confess I was disconcerted by the words "that Hotta again" and "stirred up." I didn't know how to take them. Did they mean that Hotta had stirred me up to make the disturbance bigger? Or that he had stirred up the boys in order to torment me?

As I was looking up at the blue sky, the sun gradually grew weaker and a chilly breeze sprang up. A film of cloud, like the smoke from a stick of incense, quietly spread across the surface of the limpid abyss and then was swept far, far back to become a faint mist in the depths.

"Shall we turn back?" Redshirt asked, as though it had suddenly occurred to him. Yoshikawa said that it was exactly the right time and went on to ask Redshirt if he was going to meet the Madonna that evening. Redshirt, who had been leaning over the side of the boat, straightened up a little and told him not to talk silly, because it might lead to a misunderstanding. Yoshikawa looked round at me, gave a girlish giggle and said, "It's all right. Even if he did hear . . ." I glared straight at him, my eyes flashing. He was disconcerted and looked as though he were being blinded by a bright light. Suddenly he drew in his neck, scratched his head and muttered something about surrendering. Dim-witted fool!

The boat moved across the smooth water back to the shore.

"You don't appear to like fishing very much," Redshirt remarked.

"No. I prefer lying on my back, looking up at the sky." I threw the cigarette I had been smoking into the sea. It gave a hiss and bobbed up and down on the waves that were churned up by the blade of the oar.

"All the pupils are glad to have you at the school. I hope

you'll do your best and work hard," said Redshirt, moving right away from the subject of fishing.

"I don't think they are glad."

"Oh, they are! I mean it. Very glad indeed. Isn't that right, Yoshikawa?"

"Glad isn't the word for it. They're delirious." And the Clown grinned. It was funny how every single thing he said annoyed me.

"But you'll have to be careful, you know," Redshirt went on, "or you'll be in trouble."

"Well, if there's trouble I'm ready for it," I replied. To tell the truth, I'd made up my mind that either I'd be fired or I'd make every last one of the boarders apologize. One or the other.

"Now, we'll never get anywhere if you talk like that. Don't get me wrong. I'm talking to you now as the second master; and it's for your own good."

Yoshikawa broke in to assure me that Redshirt had a high regard for me, and that he himself hoped that I would stay at the school as long as possible. He added that since we were both from Tokyo, we should help each other, and that although he didn't have much influence at the school, he was doing his best to help me. It was a rare show of human kindness on his part, but I would rather have hanged myself than be beholden to him.

"The boys really welcome your coming to the school," continued Redshirt. "But there are many factors involved. I'm sure that some things make you angry, but you should try to resign yourself to putting up with them. Believe me, I wouldn't tell you to do anything that wasn't in your best interests."

"What do you mean by 'many factors'?"

"It's rather complicated, but . . . well, you'll understand in time. You'll find out for yourself, without my explaining things to you now. Right, Yoshikawa?"

"Yes, it's all very complicated. It's not something you

71

can understand in a day or two, but you'll find out for yourself gradually, even if I don't tell you," said Yoshikawa, almost repeating what Redshirt had told me.

"Well, if things are as difficult to explain as all that, I don't want to know. I only asked because you brought the subject up."

"Yes, you're absolutely right," said Redshirt. "It's not fair to start on a subject and leave it unfinished. Well then, I'll say this much. I don't mean to be rude, but you've only just graduated and you have no experience as a teacher. There are all sorts of personal circumstances and motives to be taken into account when you're working in a school, and you can't afford to be as frank and open as when you were a student.

"Well, if I can't be frank, what can I be?"

"There you are, you see. When you're outspoken like that it shows you lack experience."

"Of course I lack experience—because I'm only twenty-three years and four months old, as I wrote on my record."

"That's my point. That's why people you would never suspect can take advantage of you."

"Providing I'm honest, I'm not afraid of anyone trying to take advantage of me."

"Of course you're not afraid. Of course not. But you *will* be taken advantage of. As a matter of fact, it happened to your predecessor. So I'm telling you, you must be careful."

It struck me that Yoshikawa had been quiet throughout all this, and when I looked round I saw that he'd slipped away to the stern and was discussing fishing with the boatman. The conversation had been far better without the Clown there.

"Who took advantage of my predecessor?"

"I can't tell you who, because that would give him a bad name. Besides, it would be wrong for me to say anything without any definite proof. Anyway, please be careful,

72

because we wouldn't want to have gone to all the trouble of getting you here for nothing."

"It's all very well to say 'be careful,' but I can't be any more careful than I am. As long as I don't do anything wrong it'll be all right, won't it?"

Redshirt laughed at this remark. I wasn't aware that I'd said anything funny. I'd only said what I'd firmly believed up to that moment. When you come to think of it, the vast majority of people encourage you to be bad. They seem to believe that, unless you are, you won't succeed in life. On the rare occasions when they see a person who is straightforward and honest, they look down on him as being green, or no better than a kid. When they teach you ethics at primary and middle school they tell you not to lie but to be honest. It would be better for the world at large but the individual himself if, instead of this, they had the courage to instruct you in methods of lying, the art of disbelieving people, and schemes for imposing on others. Redshirt had laughed at me for being innocent. What can you do in a world where innocence and frankness are laughed at? Kiyo would never have laughed at me at a time like this. She would have admired me for speaking the way I did. Kiyo·was far and away a better person than Redshirt.

"Of course it's a good thing for you not to do anything wrong; but unless you realize that even if you don't do anything wrong yourself, you can't rely on other people to do the same, you'll come to grief. Even though some people appear easygoing, some appear openhearted, and others take you into their homes and give you board and lodging, you can rarely, if ever, let your guard down, so . . .

"It's got a lot colder. Autumn's on us. Look at the shore. There's a sepia mist over it. What a lovely view! Hey!" he shouted to Yoshikawa. "Look at the shore. What do you think of that?"

"You don't often see a sight like that," agreed Yoshikawa, anxious as always to please. "I wish I had the time.

I'd like to paint it. What a pity to let a scene like that go unrecorded!"

A light came on in a second-floor room of the Minatoya; and as a train-whistle sounded, the prow of our boat ground up onto the sand. The owner of the Minatoya said, "Good evening" to Redshirt. I jumped over the side of the boat and touched the beach at last, giving a loud yell as I did so.

6

I hated the Clown. He would have been doing Japan a service if he'd tied a millstone round his neck and jumped into the sea. I didn't like Redshirt's voice. His speaking in what he considered dulcet tones was just a pose. His real voice wasn't like that at all. It didn't matter how sweet he tried to make his voice sound, with a face like his, the only woman who would fall for him was the Madonna. But, being the second master, his conversation was far more profound than the Clown's. When I got home from the fishing trip and thought over what he'd told me, there seemed to be a lot in it. Since he hadn't been specific, I couldn't really judge who he was referring to, but it did seem as though he was warning me to be on my guard against Hotta. If that was the case, why hadn't he come straight out with it? A man shouldn't insinuate. Besides, if Hotta was a bad teacher, why didn't they get rid of him straight away? Redshirt may have been a Bachelor of Arts, but he was a weakling. He had to be, because even when he was talking about someone behind his back, he didn't have the nerve to be at least honest enough to mention his name. Weaklings are always kind, which probably accounted for Redshirt's womanly gentleness. Kindness is one thing and voice another, and you can't just ignore a man's kindness because you don't like his voice. Still, it's a funny world. It's a mockery when people who disgust you are kind, and friends that you get on well with turn out to be rogues. I supposed that it was because I was in the country that everything was upside down compared to Tokyo. It was a dangerous and unsettling place. It wouldn't

75

be long, I thought, before fire froze and rocks turned into bean-curd. But Hotta didn't seem to be the kind of malicious person who would stir up the boys. It was true that he was the most popular teacher in the school and could probably have done it if he'd wanted to, but—well, first, if he'd wanted to pick a quarrel with me there was no need to choose such a roundabout way to do it. It would have been much easier to do it openly. If I were in his way he could have come to me and told me why and asked me to resign. That would have saved him a lot of time and trouble. You can work out any problem if you only discuss it. If he'd come and spoken to me and I'd thought he was right, I'd have resigned the next day. I mean, this wasn't the only place they grew rice in Japan, and wherever I went I was sure that I wouldn't die in a ditch like a beggar. I'd have thought that Hotta would have had more sense, but apparently not.

It was Hotta who had treated me to a dish of fruit-flavored ice when I first came to the school. Well, if he was as two-faced as that, I felt ashamed of accepting even that much from him. I'd only had one dish, so it had only cost him one and a half *sen*; but I'd feel bad for the rest of my life if I thought I owed one or even half a *sen* to an impostor. I decided that I'd give him back the money when I went to school the next day.

It's true that, five years before, Kiyo had lent me three yen that I'd never paid back. It wasn't that I couldn't pay, but that I wouldn't. She hadn't thought of it as a temporary loan, nor had she ever been after my money, and I had no intention of returning it and making her feel as though I looked on her as a stranger. The more I worried about such a thing, the more it would hurt Kiyo, because it would mean that I doubted her motives. It would be tantamount to accusing a wonderful person of usury.

The reason I had never repaid the money was not that I felt contempt for Kiyo but that I looked on her as my own

76

flesh and blood. There was no comparison between Kiyo and Hotta, but, whether it be a dish of crushed ice or sweet tea, if you accept something from a stranger it means that you are recognizing that person as someone of consequence and it is therefore a gesture of good will towards him or her. If you pay your share, you can of course wipe out the obligation, but the feeling of gratitude you have towards the person in whose debt you are is a far greater repayment than money can buy. I am only an ordinary man without rank or title, but I am an independent, full-fledged human being, and when an independent man takes his hat off to you, you have a gift that is worth more than a million yen. I thought I'd given Hotta that gift for the outlay of a paltry one and a half *sen*, and that he ought to be grateful. Yet he'd had the impudence to play a dirty trick on me behind my back. Right, then. The next day I'd pay him back his money, and the slate would be clean between us. Then I could pick a fight with him. Having thought things out thus far, I felt tired and fell sound asleep.

With my plan in mind, I went to school earlier than usual the next day and waited for Hotta. I waited and waited but he still didn't come. The teacher I'd nicknamed the Green Pumpkin arrived. The teacher of Chinese classics arrived. The Clown arrived. Finally even Redshirt arrived. But no Hotta. His desk was deserted except for one solitary stick of chalk lying there. I'd intended to give him the money as soon as I went into the staff room and had been clutching the one and a half *sen* in my hand all the way to school from my lodgings, just as though I were going to the bathhouse. My hands soon get sticky, and when I looked at the money I could see it was wet with sweat. I worried what Hotta would say if I gave him sweaty money, so I put the coins down on the desk, blew on them and then picked them up again.

Redshirt came up and apologized for dragging me off fishing the previous day and said that I must have found it a lot of bother. I replied that, on the contrary, I was very grateful to him for having given me such an appetite. Leaning his elbows on Hotta's desk, Redshirt brought his flat, broad, ugly face alongside my nose. Just as I was wondering what he was going to do, he asked me not to say anything to anybody about what he had told me on the way back in the boat the previous day. "You haven't mentioned it to anyone yet, have you?" he asked. His womanish voice made him sound unduly nervous. It was true that I hadn't told anybody yet, but since I intended to soon and had the money ready in my hand, I couldn't have Redshirt swearing me to secrecy now. Redshirt was Redshirt. Admittedly he hadn't mentioned Hotta by name, but I thought it irresponsible for a man in his position to pose a riddle that even I could solve and then complain when I did so. By rights, if Hotta and I were at loggerheads, he should have stepped into the thick of the fight, declared himself on my side and stuck by me till the end. If he did that it would justify his being second master and his wearing a red shirt.

When I told Redshirt that I hadn't said anything as yet but that I intended to talk to Hotta about it, he looked terribly uncomfortable and said, "You mustn't do that. It would be wrong. I don't remember saying anything specific to you about Hotta. If you do anything rash you'll put me in an extremely difficult position. You didn't come here to stir up trouble, did you?"

This seemed a strangely senseless question, so I said that naturally I had no intention of causing trouble for the school that was paying my salary.

"In that case," said Redshirt, "please keep what I told you yesterday to yourself. Don't divulge it to anyone." He was perspiring, and since he'd gone as far as to almost beg me, I said, "All right. You're putting *me* in a difficult position now, but if it means that much to you I won't say anything."

"Do you really mean it? Are you sure?" asked Redshirt, looking for reassurance. I wondered just how deep his effeminacy went and thought that it was a pretty miserable thing if all BA's were like him. He makes an unreasonable, illogical request as calmly as you please and, on top of that, when I agree he doubts my word. I'm a straightforward, honest man. If I agree to something I wouldn't dream of going back on my promise.

By now the teachers who occupied the desks on either side had arrived, and Redshirt quickly made his way back to his own place. Even his walk was affected. Whenever he walked in or out of a room he placed each foot carefully on the ground so as to make no noise. I never knew before that a noiseless walk was something to be proud of. He wasn't practicing to be a burglar, so why didn't he just walk naturally?

The bugle for the beginning of classes sounded at last. Hotta still hadn't come. There was nothing for it but to leave the money on his desk and go to the classroom.

The first class ran a little over time and I was late getting back to the teachers' room. All the other teachers were sitting at their desks, chatting. Hotta had also arrived. I'd thought he wasn't coming that day, but he'd arrived late. As soon as he saw me he said, "I ought to fine you. You made me late today." I pushed the one and a half *sen* on his desk towards him and said, "Here you are. Take this. It's for the crushed ice you bought me the other day in Tōri-chō."

"Don't be silly," he said, and began to laugh; but when he saw that I looked unexpectedly serious he told me to stop making stupid jokes and threw the money back onto my desk. Since when had porcupines started buying things for people?

"I'm not joking. I mean it. There's no reason why you should treat me to an ice, so here's the money. Is there any law that says you can't take it?"

79

"If one and a half *sen* worries you that much, I'll take it. But why didn't you return it to me before? Why now?"

"Now or any other time, it doesn't make any difference. I'm giving it to you. I don't want to be treated by you, so I'm giving you the money."

Hotta looked at me coldly and grunted. If it hadn't been for Redshirt asking me that favor I'd have told Hotta about the dirty trick he'd played, but I'd agreed to keep quiet about it. I was bright red in the face, and all Hotta could do was grunt. It wasn't reasonable.

"All right, I'll take the money for the ice, but I want you to leave your lodgings."

"All you have to do is take the money. I'll decide whether to leave my lodgings or not."

"You have no choice. The landlord came and told me yesterday that he wanted you to leave. When I heard why, I agreed with him. But to make sure, I called in there this morning to find out the details."

I didn't know what Hotta was talking about.

"How do I know what the landlord told you? You can't just decide things by yourself like that. If there's a reason, it's about time you told me. And stop being so damned rude and deciding the landlord's right straight off."

"All right then, I'll tell you. You've been so rude that they can't put up with you in the place any more. The landlady's not a maid, and it's going too far to tell her to wipe your feet for you."

"When did I make the landlady wipe my feet?"

"I don't know whether you made her or not. All I know is that they don't want you there. They said they could make the ten- or fifteen-yen rent by just selling one scroll-painting."

"Bloody cheeky pair! If that's the case, why did they take me in the first place?"

"I don't know. They just did. But they want you to leave now. Will you leave?"

80

"You bet I'll leave. I wouldn't stay now if they begged me. Why the blazes did you introduce me to a place that would use a pretext like that? It's inexcusable!"

"I wonder. Is this my fault, or because you can't behave yourself?"

Hotta had as quick a temper as I have and we were trying to shout each other down. The other people in the staff room wondered what was happening and they were all looking at us open-mouthed. I didn't consider that I'd done anything to be ashamed of. And, standing there, I swept my eyes over the whole room. Everyone except Yoshikawa looked surprised, but he just sat there smiling as though he was amused. When, however, eyes dilated, I shot a look at his long, thin face which obviously meant, "All right, you want a fight too?" he suddenly assumed a serious air and became very respectful. He looked a little scared.

A few minutes later the bugle blew. Hotta and I stopped arguing and went to our respective classrooms.

In the afternoon there was a meeting to decide how to deal with the boarders who had insulted me the night before. I'd never been to a meeting before and didn't know what it would be like. I imagined, however, that all the staff would gather together and each put his own opinions and theories forward. After this, the headmaster would sum up and then make some decision as he saw fit. This was all very well where the issues involved were not clearly black or white, but in this case, when nobody could help seeing that misconduct had been committed, I thought that a meeting was a waste of time. However you viewed the affair, it was impossible to say otherwise. In my opinion the headmaster had been very indecisive in not punishing the boys on the spot, when the facts were so cut and dried. If this was how "headmasters" behaved, then the name was nothing more nor less than another way of calling somebody weak-minded.

The meeting was held in the long, narrow room next to

the headmaster's office. Normally it served as a dining-room. About twenty chairs upholstered in black leather were arranged around the long table. The room reminded me of those rather vulgar Western-style restaurants that cater to students in Kanda in downtown Tokyo.

The headmaster sat at the head of the table and Redshirt sat next to him. The rest of us, it seemed, could sit where we wished, except that I heard the sports master always took the foot of the table out of deference. Since I didn't know the form, I squeezed myself in between the natural history master and the teacher of Chinese classics. Looking across the table, I could see Hotta and Yoshikawa seated side by side. No matter how you looked at it, Yoshikawa had an inferior face. Although we were at loggerheads, I had to admit that Hotta's was much finer. It reminded me of the face I'd seen on a scroll-painting in a room of the Yōgenji temple in Kobinata at my father's funeral. The priest told me it was Idaten, the monstrous guardian god of Buddhism. Today, because he was angry, Hotta was rolling his eyes and looking at me from time to time. If he thought he could scare me like that he was wrong. Not to be outdone, I rolled my eyes too and glared back at him. I don't have very attractive eyes, but there can be few people with eyes as big as mine. They are in fact so large that Kiyo often used to say that I ought to become an actor.

"Are we all here?" asked the headmaster. The secretary, Kawamura, began to count heads. One missing. He told this to the headmaster and tried to think who it could be. It didn't need any thinking about. Koga, the Green Pump-kin, wasn't there yet. I don't know what link of fate existed between the Pumpkin and myself, but ever since I'd first set eyes on him I couldn't get him out of my head. Whenever I walked into the staff room my eye would light on him. In fact, even on the way there he would come into my mind. When I went to the hot spring I would sometimes see his pale face bulging before me in the bath tank. If ever I said hello, he would answer in a whisper and bow with great deference. This made me feel sorry for him. Koga was the quietest person in the school. He rarely smiled, but on the other hand he didn't babble. In fact he never spoke more than was necessary. I knew the word "gentleman" from reading books, but until I met Koga I'd always thought it was just a word—something you found in a dictionary but not in real life. Now for the first time I realized that it did have a true meaning and I was filled with admiration.

Having such a deep interest in Koga, I'd noticed immediately I entered the conference room that he wasn't there. To tell the truth, I'd made him my private landmark and had thought I might sit next to him. The headmaster said that Koga would probably arrive soon and, untying a purple silk wrapper that lay in front of him, took out some mimeographed documents and began to read. Redshirt started to polish his amber pipe with a silk handkerchief. It was an obsession of his and it suited him. Some of the others were whispering to their neighbours, while those who didn't know what to do with their hands were engrossed in writing something on the table with the rubber erasers on the ends of their pencils. From time to time Yoshikawa would turn to Hotta and say something, but Hotta's only reply was an "Oh?" or an "Mm." Occasionally he shot a black look at me and, not to be outdone, I shot it straight back.

At length Koga, the man we'd all been waiting for, came in looking wretched. He apologized to the Badger very humbly and said he was sorry to be late, but that he'd had some business to attend to.

"Well then, let's start," said the Badger, and asked Kawamura, the secretary, to pass out the mimeographed sheets. Glancing at my sheet, I saw that it contained the items on the agenda. The first item was Punishment of

Offenders; the second, School Discipline; and this was followed by two or three other items. The Badger, putting on an air as always, gave the following speech as though he were the spirit of education incarnate.

"Whenever a misdemeanor is perpetrated by a teacher or pupil of this school, I take it as a reflection on my own lack of character. And whenever a regrettable incident occurs, I have a deep sense of shame that I, as headmaster, have failed to fulfill my duties. Sad to say, gentlemen, such an event has occurred—I refer to the recent disturbance—and for this I tender my most profound apologies to you all. However, what is done cannot be undone. The problem is what course of action to take. You are all conversant with the facts, and I would like you all, for my reference, to state your opinions candidly as to what remedial measures we should adopt."

In Japanese legends, badgers are supposed to be clever with their tongues. Listening to the headmaster's speech, I thought with admiration how much headmasters and badgers had in common. The headmaster had just accepted the entire responsibility, saying that it was his fault and that he was lacking in character. This seemed to indicate to me that the best course of action would be to forget about punishing the boys and for the headmaster to resign immediately. If he'd done that in the first place we wouldn't have had to go to the trouble of attending the meeting. The whole thing was just a question of common sense. I'd done my night duty quietly, and the boys had been rowdy, so it wasn't the headmaster who was at fault, nor me. The fault obviously lay with the boys and the boys alone. If Hotta had put the boys up to it then all you had to do was punish him and the boys together. One arse is a big enough burden for most people. Whoever heard of anybody saddling himself with someone else's and then going round shouting out to everyone, "This is mine. This is mine"? They say in fairy stories that badgers can change their shape. Well,

84

you'd have to be a badger to perform a contortion like that.

Having made his illogical argument, the Badger looked around the table with an air of triumph, but nobody said a word. The natural history teacher was staring at a crow perched on the roof of the school building. The teacher of Chinese classics was folding and unfolding his mimeographed sheet. Hotta was still glaring at me. If meetings were as stupid as this I'd have done better to stay away and take a nap.

I was getting annoyed, and thinking that I'd give them a good long harangue first, I was halfway out of my seat when I realized that Redshirt had begun to speak, so I subsided. Redshirt had put his pipe away and was mopping his face with a striped silk handkerchief as he spoke. He'd probably wheedled the handkerchief out of the Madonna. A man ought to use a white linen handkerchief.

"I, too, when I heard of the pupils' rowdiness felt, as second master, deeply ashamed that I had been incapable of exercising a better moral influence on these young lads. Incidents like this occur because there is a shortcoming somewhere. Now it may be that, considering the incident itself, you feel that only the pupils are at fault. It is, however, possible that, when the actual state of affairs is viewed, the responsibility may, on the contrary, lie with the school. Therefore, it is also possible that to mete out punishment, as the superficial facts seem to indicate we should, may not, in fact, be in the best future interests of the school.

"These were lusty young lads, whose natural animal spirits overflowed. Might it not be that, without thinking of right and wrong, they, half-unconsciously, committed this mischief? It is not impossible. While the course of action is, of course, entirely in the hands of the headmaster, and I have no wish to interfere, I would ask you to take these things into consideration and, using your discretion, to be as clement as possible."

It was clear that if the Badger was a badger, Redshirt was

85

no less so. He had just declared that it wasn't the boys' fault that they had misbehaved, but ours. So, apparently, if a lunatic hits somebody over the head, it's that person's fault and not the lunatic's. Thanks very much! If the kids were as full of high spirits as all that they should have gone out in the playground and wrestled with each other. If Redshirt thought that I was going to stand for having grasshoppers put "half-unconsciously" in my bed, he was wrong. The boys could half-unconsciously murder you in your sleep and Redshirt would let them off because they'd done it "half-unconsciously."

That was my opinion and I thought of saying something, but I decided that it wasn't worthwhile unless I was eloquent enough to make everyone sit up and take notice. I knew that, as always when I am angry and try to talk, I would come to a full stop after only one or two words. As people, both the Badger and Redshirt were inferior to me, but they both spoke well, and I was sure that if I made a slip while I was talking, they'd pick me up on it. I decided to form a plan, and was just composing what to say in my mind when I was surprised by Yoshikawa, sitting across the table from me, suddenly standing up. The impertinence of a clown daring to air his views! Yoshikawa spoke in his usual insincere way.

"The grasshopper incident and the whooping incident are indeed disasters which have caused all of us who wish the school well to entertain extreme misgivings about its future prosperity. We teachers must now bestir ourselves. We must reflect upon our own conduct and make the discipline for the whole school more stringent. I feel that the hypothesis which the headmaster and the second master have just propounded has gone right to the heart of the matter and is pertinent. I am therefore entirely and absolutely, and without reservation, in favor of what has been said. I would ask you to take as generous a course of action as possible."

What Yoshikawa had said was all words and no meaning. All he'd done was string a lot of long words together that made no sense. All that I'd understood was that he was entirely and absolutely, and without reservation, in favor of what had been said.

I hadn't understood what the Clown had said, but for some reason I felt very angry, so I stood up before I'd really planned what to say.

"I am entirely and absolutely, and without reservation, opposed to what has been said . . ." After that I suddenly dried up. ". . . I thoroughly dislike nonsensical, irrelevant measures." At this, the whole room burst out laughing. "The boys are solely and utterly to blame. We've simply got to make them apologize. If we don't, this kind of thing will become a habit. We must do it, even if we expel them . . . Impudence . . . They thought because I was a new teacher . . ." I sat down.

The natural history teacher, on my right, said that although undoubtedly the boys were in the wrong, if we punished them too severely we might cause a reaction and that that would never do. He added that he was in favor of being lenient, as Redshirt had suggested. Weakness! The teacher of Chinese classics, on my left, said he was in favor of settling the matter amicably. The history teacher agreed with Redshirt too. Damn! Most of them seemed to agree with Redshirt. Well, if this crowd wanted to get together and run a school, it was nothing to do with me. I washed my hands of them. But I'd decided that there were only two possible courses: either the boys apologized, or I left. And if Redshirt won I was determined to go straight back to my lodgings and pack. I knew I didn't have the ability to beat this lot in an argument anyway, and even if I did I had no desire to continue the association. I didn't care what happened to the school as long as I wasn't there. If I said anything else, they were sure to laugh at me again, so I'd be damned before I spoke.

At this point Hotta, who had listened in silence up till then, got resolutely to his feet. I had just decided that he was bound to side with the Clown and Redshirt and that, since we were on bad terms anyway, he could do what he liked, when, in a voice that made the windows rattle, he said:

"I am completely against what the second master and the other gentlemen have said. That is to say, however you view this incident, there is no getting away from the fact that fifty boarders showed contempt for a teacher who had just come to the school and that their action was designed to make a fool of him.

"Our second master seems to attribute the cause of the disturbance to the character of the teacher himself. I'm sorry if I sound rude, but I think that what he said is out of order. The teacher concerned was given night duty only twenty days after he arrived. That was too soon, because twenty days was not long enough for him to get to know the pupils. Neither, in the short space of twenty days, did the pupils have time to evaluate his character and learning. If the boys had had any just reason for feeling contempt for him, it might not be out of place to make allowances for them, but to show leniency to boys who showed such levity that, for no reason, they ridiculed a teacher who was a newcomer would, I think, undermine the school's authority and reflect on its good name.

"The word education does not merely imply the receipt of scholarship. It means the imparting of a noble, honest, chivalrous spirit, and the eradication of sneaky, flippant and insolent habits. The day we temporize because we are afraid of reaction or fear that a disturbance will grow is the day we will not be able to remedy those bad habits. The reason we are here in this school is to put a stop to bad habits, and it is my opinion that if we are going to overlook an incident such as this, we should not have become teachers in the first place. I think, then, that the right course would be to punish all the boarders severely and to make them apologize publicly to the teacher concerned." With that, Hotta let himself drop onto his chair with a bang.

Everyone remained absolutely quiet. Redshirt began to polish his pipe again. I was very happy. It was just as though Hotta had said everything for me that I wanted to say. I'm a simple person, and with an expression on my face that showed I'd forgotten our quarrel and was grateful, I looked across at Hotta as he sat there. He completely ignored me.

After a few moments Hotta stood up again. "I'd like to add something that I forgot to say just now. It appears that on the night in question the teacher on night duty left the school and went to a hot spring. I think that was inexcusable. Even if he didn't like the duty, it was his responsibility to look after the school while everyone else was away. It is disgraceful that, because there was no one to stop him, he should have gone to a hot spring, or anywhere else for that matter. Leaving aside the question of the boys, I sincerely hope that the headmaster will reprimand the person responsible for his neglect of duty."

Hotta was a funny person. No sooner had he praised you than he was revealing your mistakes. I knew the person on duty before me had gone out, and I went to the hot spring because I thought that that was the custom. Now I realized by what Hotta said that I'd been wrong and I thought that it was only natural that I be attacked for it. I got to my feet again and said, "It's quite true that I went to the hot spring while I was on night duty. That was very wrong of me. I apologize."

As I sat down everyone began to laugh. "Useless lot! If *you* were wrong could you stand up and admit it in public? Of course you couldn't. That's why you're laughing," I thought.

The headmaster then stood up and said that as it seemed

there were no further opinions, he would decide what to do after careful consideration.

The result, by the way, was that the boarders were confined to the school for a week and had to come to me and apologize. If they hadn't apologized I'd intended to hand in my certificate of appointment and go home, but since they more or less did what I wanted, I stayed—a fact which lead to a great deal of trouble, but I'll tell you about that later.

The headmaster, still as part of the meeting, then said, "We teachers must correct the behavior of the pupils by example. As a first step towards that end I would appreciate it if teachers would please refrain as far as possible from frequenting bars and restaurants. I except, of course, occasions such as farewell parties, but I would like you to stop going alone to low places—for example, noodle shops and dumpling shops."

This was again the signal for general laughter. The Clown winked at Hotta and said, "Fried prawns," but Hotta took no notice. Served the Clown right!

Not being very bright, I didn't fully grasp what the Badger was on about, but I thought that if a middle-school teacher couldn't go to a noodle or a dumpling shop then the job was no good for someone with my appetite. That was fine. But if that was the case why hadn't the school advertised for a person who didn't like noodles or dumplings from the very beginning? The Badger had given me my certificate of appointment without a word about any of this, and it came as a terrible blow to a man like me, with no other interests, to have someone suddenly issue the unfair proclamation that you mustn't eat noodles and you mustn't eat dumplings. Redshirt spoke again. "Middle-school teachers belong to the upper echelons of society and should therefore not merely seek after material pleasures, for, if indulged in, they will eventually have a bad effect on one's character. However, being human, we could not possibly live in a small country place such as this without some form of amusement. We should, therefore, seek some elevated spiritual recreation such as fishing, reading works of literature, or composing modern poetry or classical *haiku* poems . . ." Redshirt took advantage of the fact that everyone was listening in silence to give his tongue free play.

If going out to sea and fishing for fertilizer, a *goruki* becoming a Russian writer, your favourite geisha standing under a pine tree, and poems about old ponds and frogs[2] were spiritual and mental recreation, then so was eating fried prawns and dumplings. Instead of bestowing recreation like that on people, Redshirt would have done better to stay at home and do his washing.

I was so angry that I asked, "Is meeting the Madonna spiritual recreation?"

This time nobody laughed. They just looked at one another with odd expressions on their faces. Redshirt himself had his head bent and looked as though he was in pain. Take that! That one went home! The only thing I felt sorry about was that when I mentioned the Madonna, Koga's pale pumpkin face grew paler than ever.

7

I'd gone home and was packing my things when the landlady came and asked me if anything was wrong. She said that if something had happened to make me angry she would put it right if I would tell her what it was. This took me by surprise. Why, I wondered, was the world full of such inconsistent people? I didn't know whether she wanted me to leave or to stay. She was out of her mind. Thinking that it was beneath the dignity of a Tokyoite to argue with a woman like her, I went and called a rickshaw and was out of the place in no time.

I'd left my lodgings, but I had no idea where to go.

"Where to, sir?" the rickshaw-man asked.

"Just shut up and follow me. You'll soon find out," I answered, and set off at a brisk pace. To save a lot of trouble I thought of going back to the Yamashiroya, until I realized that I would, in fact, be causing myself more bother if I did so, because my money wouldn't allow me to stay there long and I'd have to move again. I thought that, walking along as I was, I might see a notice for room and board or something. If I did I'd take it as a providential sign and move in.

I was strolling round a quiet neighborhood that looked as though it would be nice to live in, when I came out at a place called Kajiyachō. This was an area of large residences belonging to samurai families and wasn't a place where you'd be likely to find lodgings. I was about to retrace my steps and head for a busier, more lively part of town, when the thought quite suddenly struck me that this was where Koga, the teacher I had such a high regard for, lived. He had been born and bred in the place and his family had owned a large house here for generations. He must be well acquainted with the district. Perhaps if I went and asked him he would be able to tell me of a suitable place where I could stay. Fortunately, I'd dropped in to say hello once before and knew where he lived, so I was spared the trouble of having to traipse around hunting for his house.

I walked up to what I'd decided looked like the place and called out, "Excuse me." I had to call twice before an elderly woman of about fifty came out from inside the house, carrying a small, old-fashioned night-light with a paper shade. Not that I'm averse to young women, but whenever I see an elderly woman it always makes me feel nostalgic. It's probably because of my fondness for Kiyo. I expect my feelings for her transfer themselves to every other old lady I see.

The woman carrying the night-light was, I presumed, Koga's mother. She was a dignified woman and wore her hair, as widows do, down, and neatly trimmed. There was a strong resemblance between her and Koga. She invited me in, but when I told her that I only wanted to see her son for a moment, she called him to the door. I explained the circumstances and asked him whether he had any suggestions.

"Oh, my! You are in a fix, aren't you?" he said. Then, after thinking for a while: "There's an old couple called Hagino who live by themselves in one of the poorer, back-street areas behind here. They told me the other day that they have a room empty, just going to waste. They said they'd let it if they could find a gentleman to take it and asked me if I could recommend anyone. I don't know if they're still of the same mind, but anyway let's go and ask." He then very kindly took me to their house.

From that evening I became a boarder in the Hagino house. What surprised me, though, was that the day after I left Ikagin's place Yoshikawa moved in and occupied my old room as if it had been the most natural thing in the world. Even I was taken aback by this. It seemed as though the world was composed entirely of crooks, all waiting for a chance to take advantage of one another. I was disgusted.

If that's the way the world is, I thought, the only way to get by is to behave the same as everybody else. But if I couldn't get three meals a day without stooping to the level of the scum who take a rake-off from pickpockets, I'd have to seriously think about suicide, though for me to have hanged myself while I was in sound health would have been an insult to my ancestors and wouldn't have looked good. On reflection, it seemed to me that I would have been better off if I'd used my six hundred yen as capital and started up as a milkman or something, instead of having gone to the School of Physics and studying an absolutely useless subject like mathematics. If I had, Kiyo would have been able to stay with me and I wouldn't have had to worry how the old lady was getting on miles away. I hadn't thought so when we were together, but now that I'd come away to the country I realized what a wonderful person Kiyo was. You could search the length and breadth of Japan and you'd seldom find such a good-natured woman. When I'd left Tokyo she'd had a slight cold, and I wondered how she was now. I imagined that she'd been very happy to receive the letter I'd written to her a while ago. I should be hearing from her soon. For two or three days I thought of nothing else.

It was beginning to prey on my mind, and from time to time I would ask my landlady if there was a letter for me from Tokyo. But, every time, she would give me a pitying look and reply that there wasn't.

My present landlord and his wife were very different from the Ikagins. They both came from samurai families and were very refined. Admittedly I was annoyed in the evenings by the old man chanting Japanese lyrical dramas in a peculiar voice, but that was a lot better than having

94

Ikagin constantly offering to brew me up a nice cup of tea.

Sometimes the old lady would come to my room and chat about all manner of things and ask me questions: why, for instance, I hadn't brought my wife along with me? I asked her if I looked old enough to have a wife and told her that, though I might not look it, I was—Lord help me!—only twenty-four.

She began by telling me that it was only right and proper for a man to have a wife at twenty-four and then went on to give me half a dozen examples of people who were married at twenty and the father of two children at twenty-two. I didn't know how to contradict her, so, copying her dialect, I said that, being twenty-four, I'd like to get married and would she please find a wife for me?

"Are you really serious?" the old lady asked.

"Serious? Of course I'm serious. I'm just dying to get married."

"Yes, you would be, like. Everyone is when they're young." This sally caught me off guard and I didn't know what to say.

"But you know, sir, I'm sure you've got a wife. I can tell by the look of you."

"Ah, you're very perceptive. How did you know?"

"How did I know? Why, because you come to me in a fever every day and ask if there's a letter from Tokyo."

"Well I never! Such perception!"

"I'm right, aren't I?"

"Well, you may be."

"But young girls nowadays aren't like they used to be. You have to watch 'em. You'd better be careful."

"What? You mean my wife's having an affair with someone in Tokyo?"

"Oh no! *Your* wife's all right, but . . ."

"Thank goodness for that. But, if that's the case, what is there to be careful about?"

"Your wife's all right—yes, *she*'s all right, but . . ."

"Well, is there someone who isn't?"

"There's a lot hereabouts. Do you know Tōyama's daughter, sir?"

"No, I'm afraid not."

"You don't know her yet? Why, bless you, she's the prettiest girl in these parts. She's so beautiful all the teachers at the school call her the Madonna. You haven't heard of her yet?"

"Oh, the Madonna? I thought that was the name of a geisha."

"Good gracious, no! Madonna is what foreigners call a beautiful woman, I think."

"Yes, that's possible. Well, well, well!"

"I expect the art master gave her that name."

"Who? The Clown?"

"No. That Yoshikawa. He gave it to her."

"And is the Madonna unreliable?"

"That Madonna's not a madonna to be trusted."

"Well, there's a fine state of affairs. But you could be right about the Madonna. There's never been a decent woman with a nickname yet."

"That's true. Think of those characters in Kabuki plays. There's O-matsu, that they called the devil, and Dakki no O-hyaku—they were both dreadful women."

"Is the Madonna like them?"

"Ah, that Madonna. Well, she and Mr. Koga—the gentleman that so kindly brought you here—were engaged."

"Really? Well I'll be . . . Who'd have thought that the Pumpkin was as lucky in love as all that? You can't go by appearances, can you? I must be a bit more careful in the future."

"Anyway, last year Mr. Koga's father died—the family had had money before that, and shares in a bank. Everything had gone very nicely up till then, but when he died things started going badly for them for some reason.

What I mean is, Mr. Koga's such an easy person and he's being imposed on. The Madonna's family kept postponing the wedding for one reason and another, and then the second master at the school said that he wanted the Madonna to be his wife."

"You mean Redshirt? He's a real so-and-so. I thought that shirt of his wasn't an ordinary one. Well, what happened then?"

"He asked someone he knew to make the proposal to the Tōyamas, but they felt a sense of obligation to Mr. Koga and said they couldn't give him an answer immediately— they said they'd give the matter careful thought, or something like that. After that, Redshirt was in and out of their place trying to persuade them, until he eventually managed to win the young lady over. Redshirt was in the wrong of course, but so was the Madonna. Nobody has a good word for her. She accepted Mr. Koga's proposal and then, as soon as this scholar came along, she switched to him. It's outrageous. It's an insult to the god who watches over us today."

"You're quite right. It's an insult to the god of today, tomorrow, the day after tomorrow, or any other day for that matter."

"Mr. Hotta, who's a friend of Mr. Koga's and felt sorry for him, went to the second master and told him what he thought of his behavior. Redshirt said that he had no intention of trying to steal somebody who was already engaged, but if the engagement should be broken he might marry the Madonna, and that his calls were just friendly, social ones on the whole Tōyama family. He said that he didn't see what harm social calls on the Tōyamas did to Mr. Koga. Mr. Hotta had no choice but to accept what he said. They say there's been bad blood between Redshirt and Mr. Hotta ever since."

"You seem to know about everything. How did you find out all the details? I'm impressed."

"This place is too small to keep a secret in."

She knew too much for my liking. It was possible she'd even heard about the business of the fried prawns and the dumplings. This was a troublesome place, but it had its compensations. I'd found out the meaning of Madonna, and the information about the relationship between Hotta and Redshirt was very enlightening. The only thing that bothered me now was that it wasn't clear which of them was in the wrong. I'm such a simple person that unless things are clearly labeled black and white, I don't know whose side to take.

"Who do you think is the better person, Redshirt or the Porcupine?"

"What do you mean by 'porcupine'?"

"Porcupine? Oh, that's Hotta."

"Well Mr. Hotta's certainly the stronger of the two, but Redshirt's a scholar and is the more able. And then, when it comes to being kind, Redshirt's kinder; but they say Mr. Hotta is more popular with the pupils."

"So which one is the better?"

"I suppose the one that earns more money is the greater person."

I was obviously getting nowhere with this line of inquiry, so I stopped.

Two or three days later, when I arrived home from school, the old lady gave me a broad grin and said the letter I'd been waiting for had come at last. She put the letter down and, telling me to read it carefully, left the room. When she'd gone I picked it up and saw that it was from Kiyo. The envelope had two or three slips of paper stuck on it and a closer examination revealed that the letter had been sent from the Yamashiroya to Ikagin's house and from there to the Haginos'. Moreover, it seemed that the letter had been at the Yamashiroya for about a week. They apparently took their duties as an inn seriously: it wasn't only people that lodged there but letters too.

I opened the letter and found that it was very long. This is what it said:

My Dear Botchan,

I was going to answer your letter right away but I unfortunately had a cold which kept me in bed for a week so I couldn't. I'm sorry it's so late. On top of that I'm afraid I can't read and write as well as the young ladies nowadays and it took me a lot of time and trouble to write this even though I know the writing is still bad. I thought of asking my nephew to write the letter for me but I thought that if I was going to send you a letter it would be rude not to write it myself so I wrote it out roughly first then copied it properly. I finished the copy in two days but it took me four days to write it out roughly. You may find it difficult to read but I took a lot of trouble over it so please read it to the end.

After this introduction, the letter went on for about four feet, talking of this and that. She was right, it was difficult to read. It wasn't only that the writing was bad. She'd used very few Chinese characters and had written for the most part in the *hiragana* syllabary, so it was a terrible job to work out where one word ended and another began.

I'm very impatient by nature and normally I wouldn't read a long, badly-written letter like that even if somebody offered me five yen to do it, but just this once I forced myself to be patient and read it through from beginning to end. I should add, however, that although I read it, I had such a lot of trouble making out the words that I didn't get any of the meaning and had to read it through from the beginning all over again.

It had grown rather dark inside the room and for some time it had been difficult to read, so at length I went out and sat on the edge of the verandah and read the letter through carefully. An early-autumn wind shook the banana plants in the garden, passed over the exposed parts of my body and returned to make the letter I had started to re-read flutter like a pennant in my hands and stream out at

99

. . . I went out and sat on the edge of the verandah and read the letter through carefully.

the garden. The four or more feet of paper finally began to flap so much that I thought if I released it it might fly across to the hedge opposite. But I was too busy reading to indulge in such fancies for long.

Kiyo's letter continued:

You have always been a frank and honest person but I'm worried about your being too quick-tempered. You mustn't go around giving people nicknames left and right, it will make them dislike you. If you must give people nicknames then only use them in your letters to me. —They say that country people are bad so be careful that nothing happens to you. —I'm sure the weather there is a lot less reliable than in Tokyo so wrap up well when you go to bed and don't catch a chill. Your letter was too short for me to know much about what things are like there so next time please write a letter at least half as long as this one. —It was all right to give the people at the inn a five-yen tip but won't you find yourself short later? Money is the only thing you can rely on when you're in the country so you must look after your money and put aside as much as you can for a rainy day. —I thought you might be short of pocket-money so I'm sending you a ten-yen money order. I put the fifty yen you gave me the other day in postal savings. I thought that it would be a help when you come back to Tokyo and get a house of your own. Even without this ten yen there's forty left so don't worry.

Thrift, thy name is woman!

I was sitting on the edge of the verandah, deep in thought, allowing Kiyo's letter to flutter in the breeze, when old Mrs. Hagino slid back the partition and came into the room carrying my supper.

"Are you still reading your letter? It must really be a long one."

"Yes. It's a very important letter, so I let it blow in the wind, then read it, then let it blow in the wind again, then read it again," I replied, not understanding what I meant myself. I then sat down to supper. Boiled sweet potatoes again! The Haginos were politer, kinder and more refined than the Ikagins, but, unfortunately, the food there was bad. We'd had potatoes the night before and the night before that, and now we had them again this evening. Admittedly I had said I loved potatoes, but I couldn't survive on potatoes alone, day in and day out. Instead of me laughing at Koga and calling him the Green Pumpkin, people would soon be laughing at me and calling me the Pale Potato. If Kiyo had been there, she'd have prepared some of the slices of raw tunny that I love, or some hashed fish broiled in soy, but there was no hope of any such thing from a poor, tightfisted samurai family like the Haginos.

However you looked at it, I couldn't get along without Kiyo. If it seemed as though I was going to stay at the school for any length of time, I'd bring her down from Tokyo. It's a hard thing when an educator of boys has to become sallow because he mustn't eat fried prawns with noodles, he mustn't eat rice dumplings, and then, when he returns to his lodgings, all he gets is potatoes. I imagined that even the ascetic priests of the Zen sect had more delicacies to eat than that. I polished off the plateful of potatoes and then, taking two raw eggs from a drawer in the desk, I cracked them on the rim of my rice bowl and swallowed them—thus, at least, managing to stave off death by starvation for the time being. Without the nourishment from raw eggs, I would never have had the strength to teach for twenty-one hours a week.

Kiyo's letter had made me late going to the hot spring for a bath. Having been every day, however, it had become a habit with me and I wouldn't have felt right if I'd missed even one day. Thinking that I'd take the train, I set off for the station with, as always, my red towel hanging from my hand. I arrived at the station two or three minutes after a train had gone, and there was a little while to wait before the next one. I had sat down on a bench and begun to smoke a *Shikishima* when who should come along but

Koga. I felt even more sorry for him, now that I'd heard the story from Mrs. Hagino. He always looked the picture of misery, trying as he did to make himself appear small, as though he considered himself a parasite crawling between heaven and earth. But this evening was no time to simply pity him. If it had been possible, I'd have liked to double his salary, see him married to the Tōyama girl the next day, and send them off for a month's holiday to Tokyo.

Being in this frame of mind I said, "Hello there! Off to the bath? Here, sit down," and promptly moved over to make room for him. He looked very humble and said, "No, thank you. Please don't bother," and out of modesty, or some such scruple, continued to stand.

"There's still a while to wait. You'll get tired. Come on, sit down," I said, repeating the invitation. I felt so painfully sorry for him that I wanted to have him sit next to me.

"Well then, perhaps I will. Excuse me." With this he at last gave in and sat down.

There are in this world insolent people like the Clown who'll thrust themselves in where they're not wanted. Others, like Hotta, go around with a look on their face which plainly shows that they think the country would collapse without them. On the other hand, there are the Redshirts of the world who, in their vanity, set themselves up as the monopolizers of cosmetics and dandyism, and people like the Badger who think they are education incarnate, in a frock coat. Everyone feels superior in his own way. I'd never met a person as self-effacing as Koga. It was almost as though he wasn't there. He had the air of a pawned doll. His face was bloated, it's true, but I couldn't understand anyone giving up a fine person like him for someone like Redshirt. If that's what the Madonna intended to do she must be a shameless coquette. As a husband, Koga would be worth more than a gross of Redshirts.

"Are you ill? You look very tired."

"No, there's nothing specially wrong with me."

"Oh, good. A man's nothing without his health, is he?"

"You seem to be very fit."

"Yes. I'm thin, but I'm never ill. I hate illness, you see."
Koga grinned at this.

At that moment the sound of a young woman's laughter came from the direction of the entrance. When I glanced round, there stood a fantastic woman. She was tall and lovely, with beautiful white skin and her hair dressed in the height of fashion. She was standing in front of the ticket-window with a woman of about forty-five or -six. It's beyond my power to describe beautiful women, but there's no doubt that she was lovely. When I saw her I felt as though I were holding in my hand a smooth piece of crystal, steeped in warm perfume. The older woman was shorter than the young one, but there was a close facial resemblance and I guessed that they were mother and daughter.

No sooner had I become aware of the woman's presence than I forgot all about Koga and kept my eyes on her. Suddenly Koga stood up beside me and walked timidly across towards the two women. This surprised me a little. The young girl must be the Madonna, I thought. The three of them stood in front of the booking office, exchanging a few words of greeting, but I was too far away to hear what was said.

Looking up at the station clock, I saw that the next train was due to leave the station in another five minutes. I wished it would hurry up and come. I had no one to talk to now and was beginning to get impatient. Just then another figure came dashing into the station. It was Red-shirt. He was wearing a thin, unlined kimono, tied slovenly around the waist with a crepe sash. As always, he was wearing his gold watch chain. Actually it wasn't really gold. Redshirt thought that nobody knew and was always showing if off. But I knew.

As Redshirt rushed into the station, he cast an inquiring

It's beyond my power to describe beautiful women, but there's no doubt that she was lovely.

glance around, as though he was looking for somebody or something, then went up and bowed politely to the three talking at the booking office. Having said one or two words to them, he suddenly turned in my direction and, catfooted as ever, padded over to me.

"Hello. You going for a bath too? I was worried that I'd miss the train. I hurried all the way. We still have three minutes. I wonder if that clock's right?" He pulled out his own gold watch and, remarking that the clock was two minutes off, sat down beside me. He never once looked across at the women but stared straight in front of him, with his chin resting on the head of his walking stick. From time to time the older woman glanced in Redshirt's direction, but the young one remained turned away.

Eventually, with a whistle from it's engine, the train drew up to the platform. Everyone who had been waiting streamed on, and it was every man for himself. Redshirt leaped into the first-class carriage ahead of anyone else. There was nothing to be proud of in traveling first class. There were only two classes: first and second. The first-class fare was five *sen* and the second-class fare was three *sen*, so a mere two *sen* stood between an first-class man and a second. When I tell you that even I could afford to pay out the money for a white first-class ticket, you'll understand what I mean. All country people, however, are tightfisted—even two *sen* more or less is a matter of great concern to them—and most of them went second class.

The Madonna and her mother followed Redshirt into the first-class carriage. Koga always went second class. It was as though it were second nature to him. He stood hesitating in front of the second-class coach, then, catching sight of me, he seemed to make up his mind and jumped aboard. I felt so sorry for him that I immediately got into the same carriage after him. I presumed that no one would mind me going second class with a first-class ticket.

At the hot spring, I came down to the bath tank from

the third floor in my bathrobe and met Koga once again. When I try to speak at committee meetings or on other formal occasions, my throat seizes up at the last minute and nothing comes out, but usually I'm a great talker and I tried to strike up a conversation with Koga in the bath tank. He looked unbearably pathetic. I thought that as a Tokyoite it was my duty to offer a word of cheer and comfort at times like this. Unfortunately, however, Koga wouldn't follow my lead. He just couldn't get into the spirit of the thing. No matter what I said, he just answered yes or no, and as even that much seemed an effort, I finally shut up and excused myself.

I didn't meet Redshirt in the bath. But there were many bathhouses, and just because we'd come on the same train was no reason to think that we'd necessarily meet in the same bath tank. I didn't think it in the least strange.

When I left the hot-spring hotel I was greeted by a beautiful moon. The branches of the willows growing on either side of the street cast round shadows onto the roadway. I decided to go for a stroll and walked uphill to the north until I came to the outskirts of the town. There, on the left, was a large gate and at the end of the street which led away from the gate stood a Buddhist temple. The street was lined with brothels. I thought that having a red-light quarter inside a temple gate must be a hitherto unheard-of phenomenon. I would have liked to go and have a look, but the thought that I might get into trouble with the Badger again, as I had at the meeting, stopped me and I walked straight past.

On the same side of the road as the temple gate, and a little farther on, was a one-story building with a black half-curtain across the doorway, and a small lattice window. This was the shop where I'd made the mistake of eating dumplings. The round lantern hanging outside announced that they served *shiruko*—red-bean soup with rice-cake in it—and *o-zōni*—vegetables and rice-cake boiled in soy. The light from the lantern fell on the trunk of a willow tree that stood near the eaves. I wanted to go in for something to eat, but I restrained myself and walked on.

It's hard not to be able to eat dumplings when you want to, but I suppose it's harder still to have your fiancée leave you for someone else. When I considered what Koga was suffering, I thought that going without dumplings for three days, or even any food at all for that matter, wouldn't be much to complain about.

There's nothing so unreliable as people. You'd never have thought, looking at the Madonna's face, that she'd have been capable of being so heartless, but, nevertheless, there she was, a beautiful woman, being cruel. And there was Koga, with a face like a white pumpkin distended with water, a good, kind man and a gentleman. It never pays to take anyone at face value.

I'd thought that Hotta was straight, with no nonsense about him, and then they'd said he'd incited the pupils. But just when I'd accepted that he had done so, he'd pressed the headmaster to punish the boys.

Redshirt, who was the embodiment of offensiveness, had been unexpectedly kind and warned me to be on my guard, although I was nothing to him. Then he'd hoodwinked the Madonna—or I'd thought he had. But then I'd heard that he only wanted to marry her in the event of her engagement to Koga being broken off.

Ikagin had found fault with me and thrown me out, but moved the Clown in in my place. No matter how you look at it, there's nothing so unreliable as people. If I'd written to Kiyo and told her of all these goings-on I'm sure she would have been astounded. She, as a Tokyoite, would probably have said that the place was a den of thieves because it lay beyond Hakone.

It isn't in my nature to worry about the future and I've never let anything that's happened bother me; I've just gone on getting by from day to day. I must confess, however, that in the month, or maybe less, that I had been in that place, I had come to look on the world as a dangerous place. Although nothing spectacular had happened to me in that time, I felt as though I'd been there for five or six years. It seemed that the best thing I could do was to leave as soon as possible and go back to Tokyo.

Thought after thought ran through my mind, one leading to the other, until at last I crossed a stone bridge and found myself on the far bank of the river Nozeri. I say river, but that's too good a word for it. It was in fact a little rippling brook about six feet wide. If you followed the bank for about three-quarters of a mile downstream, you came to the village of Aioi. There is a statue of Kannon, the goddess of mercy, in this village.

Looking back at the hot-spring town, I could see red lights shining in the moonlight. I could also hear the sound of drums coming, I was sure, from the brothel quarter. Though shallow, the stream flowed along swiftly and sparkled and glittered nervously as it caught the light. I had been strolling along the top of the bank for what, I judged, must have been a quarter of a mile, when I saw what looked like someone walking ahead of me. With the aid of the moonlight, I was able to make out two shadowy figures. Possibly two young lads on their way back to the village from the hot spring. If they were though, it was strange that they weren't singing. They were unusually quiet.

As I continued on, it seemed that I was walking quicker than they were and the two shadows gradually grew larger. One looked like a woman. I was about thirty yards behind them when the man, catching the sound of my footsteps, spun round. The moon was shining from behind me. I caught a glimpse of him and thought, "Could it be?" The man and the woman resumed their walk, but I had an idea and set off after them as fast as I could.

They walked on at the same leisurely pace as before,

109

As I continued on, it seemed that I was walking quicker than they were and the two shadows gradually grew larger.

unaware that they were being followed. I was now so close to them that I could distinctly hear every word they said. The path along the top of the bank was about six feet wide, scarcely room for three people to walk abreast. I easily overtook the couple, brushing the man's sleeve as I did so. Two steps ahead of them, I turned on my heel and stared at the man's face. The moon shone full and unrestrainedly on my face. It lit up everything from my close-cropped hair to my chin. The man gave a suppressed cry of surprise, suddenly swung towards the woman and hurriedly suggested they should turn back. Then they both headed back towards the hot-spring town.

I wondered whether Redshirt had the effrontery to think he could fool me, or whether he was too chickenhearted to speak up and admit it was him. Anyway, it seemed that I wasn't the only one to find the place too small for comfort.

8

I had begun to suspect Hotta after I came back from the fishing trip to which Redshirt had invited me. Being told by him to leave my lodgings on the merest pretext had confirmed me in my opinion that he was a rogue. I was puzzled, however, by his having spoken out so strongly in favor of punishing the boys severely. That had been unexpected. When old Mrs. Hagino told me that Hotta had been to have a talk with Redshirt about Koga, I had thought it was an admirable thing to do. On the other hand, the circumstances seemed to indicate that it was Redshirt, and not Hotta, who was the rogue—that Redshirt had indirectly filled my head with a lot of spurious information dressed up to look like the truth. I'd been confused about the whole thing. But since seeing Redshirt walking with the Madonna beside the Nozeri river, I'd become convinced that he was an old fox. I wasn't sure whether he was a crook or not, but he certainly wasn't a nice person. He was two-faced. You can't trust a man unless he's as straight as a die.

If a man's straight it's a pleasure to fight with him, but you have to watch a man who's all sweetness and light, refined, and shows off his amber pipe in a self-satisfied way. You'd have to be careful when and how you fought him. Even if you did pick a quarrel with such a man you couldn't have such a pleasant fight as you see the sumo wrestlers at the Ekōin temple having. Hotta, with whom I'd shocked the whole staff room by arguing about who was to have the one and a half *sen*, was far more human. I'd disliked Hotta when he'd glared at me in the meeting with his round, deep-set eyes, but thinking about it afterwards I'd decided I preferred Hotta's eyes to Redshirt's garrulous, insinuating voice. As a matter of fact, I had started to speak to Hotta after the meeting, thinking I'd make up our quarrel. He had just turned those eyes of his on me without a word, and then I'd got angry and left things as they were.

 • Since then Hotta and I hadn't spoken to each other. The one and a half *sen* that I'd put on his desk still lay there— now covered with dust. I, of course, wasn't going to do anything about it, and Hotta steadfastly refused to pick it up. Those coins had become a barrier between us. I couldn't speak to him even if I wanted to, and he maintained a dogged silence. That one and a half *sen* was a curse on both of us. It had finally become painful to go to school and see the coins.

While relations between Hotta and myself had been severed, Redshirt and I still continued on the same terms as before. The day after I saw him beside the Nozeri river he hurried across to me at school, sat down beside me and began talking of this and that: how were my new lodgings? —and how about going fishing for Russian literature again? My feelings towards him at the time being not exactly pleasant, I remarked that I'd seen him twice the previous evening.

"Yes," he replied. "At the station—do you always go out at that time? It's rather late, isn't it?"

When I hit him with the information that I'd also seen him beside the Nozeri river, he said that he hadn't been there, and that he'd come straight home after his bath. What was the point of his trying to conceal it? I *had* seen him there and that was a fact. He was always lying. If he could be the second master in a middle school, I could be the president of a university. From then on I ceased to trust Redshirt. The world's a strange place. I was on speaking terms with Redshirt, whom I didn't trust, and not with Hotta, whom I admired.

One day Redshirt asked me if I'd call at his home, as he had something to talk to me about. I thought it a pity that I'd have to miss going to the hot spring, but I left for his place at about four o'clock.

Redshirt was a bachelor, but, being second master, he had long ago moved out of lodgings and now lived in a fine house with an imposing portico. I'd heard that the rent was nine and a half yen. It had such a fine entrance that I thought if you could rent a house like that in the country for nine and a half yen, I might send for Kiyo from Tokyo. She would have been delighted with such a place.

I called out from the porch, and Redshirt's young brother came to the door. I was teaching the brother algebra and arithmetic at school. He was useless. He had, however, lived in various places and seen something of life and had a far worse character than the boys who had been born and brought up in the country. When I met Redshirt and asked him what it was he wanted to talk to me about, his nibs, smoking some foul tobacco that smelled like quinine in his amber pipe, said, "Since you arrived, we've had better results than in your predecessor's time. The headmaster is very pleased. He feels that we were very lucky to get you. Since we at the school have such faith in you, I'd like you to make a real effort and do your best."

"I see. But I can't do any better than I am."

"Just carry on as you are. That will be fine. But I hope you won't forget the little talk we had the other day."

"You mean about people who find you lodgings being dangerous?"

"You mustn't be so outspoken, or the whole thing will be pointless . . . Anyway, that's all right; I am sure you are well aware of what I mean. If you continue making the effort you have been—the school notices things, you know —I think that in a little while, when the time is ripe, we may be able to do a little something about your remuneration."

114

"You mean my salary?" I asked in surprise. "I'm not worried about my salary, but, of course, I'd rather have it go up than not."

"Fortunately one of the teachers is going to be transferred to another school and, while naturally I can't make any promises without consulting the headmaster, it's possible that we might be able to spare you a little from his salary. Anyhow, that's what I'm thinking of asking the headmaster to do."

"Thank you very much. Who's going to be transferred?"

"It'll be announced soon anyway, so I don't suppose there's any harm in telling you. As a matter of fact, it's Koga."

"Mr. Koga? But he's lived here all his life."

"That's true, but there are circumstances—it's partly his own wish."

"Where's he going to?"

"To Nobeoka, in Hyūga province. Because of the inconvenience of the place, he'll be going there with a better salary."

"Who's going to take his place?"

"We have someone in mind and it's about settled. He's coming on terms that will make it possible to increase your salary."

"That's wonderful. But you don't have to raise it if it's going to cause problems."

"At any rate, I intend to talk to the headmaster about it. I think he agrees with me, but we may have to ask you to work more later on, so please be prepared to do so."

"You mean I'll have to work more hours?"

"No, your hours may be less."

"That seems strange. Less hours but more work."

"Yes, it does seem strange, I agree. It's rather difficult to be specific now, but—well, what I mean is, we may ask you to take on greater responsibility."

I was completely at sea. When he said "greater responsibility" I imagined he was referring to being head of the mathematics department. But that was Hotta's job and I was sure he had no idea of resigning. Also, being the most popular teacher in the school, I couldn't see them planning to transfer or fire him. There was always a kind of fog around everything Redshirt said. Understand him or not, however, he had apparently finished telling me what he had to. We carried on a desultory conversation for a while, in the course of which Redshirt told me about the farewell party they were going to hold for Koga, asked me if I drank, and remarked that Koga was a gentleman who deserved everyone's affection. Finally, changing the subject, he asked me if I wrote *haiku*. Here comes trouble, I thought, and replying no, I didn't write *haiku*, I said goodbye and left hastily. *Haiku* are for Bashō or dilettantes with plenty of time on their hands. There's a poem which talks about morning-glory creepers entwined about the rope of a well-bucket.[3] Well, you won't catch a mathematics teacher becoming entangled with *haiku* like that.

When I arrived home I fell to thinking. There were, I thought, some incomprehensible people in the world. Why would a man who owned a large house and taught in a school which was ideal for him in every way say that he was tired of the place where he had been born and bred and deliberately look for problems by going to a strange province that he knew nothing about? It would have been different if he had been going to a fine place, like Tokyo, that had trains and trams. But Nobeoka, in Hyūga province? The place where we were had a good boat service, and I even wanted to leave *there* after less than a month. Nobeoka lies deep in the heart of the mountains, beyond range after range. According to Redshirt, when you got off the boat it took a day by horse-and-cart to Mizaki. From Mizaki the only way to reach Nobeoka was by rickshaw. That took another day. The very name sounded uncivilized. It made you imagine a place populated half by monkeys and half by men. I knew Koga was saint-like and acted like a sage, but what possible vagary could have possessed him that he should want to go and keep company with monkeys?

While I was thinking, the old lady brought in supper as usual. I asked her if we had potatoes again, but she said no, this evening it was bean-curd. Potatoes or bean-curd, there isn't much difference.

"I hear that Mr. Koga's going to Hyūga."

"Yes, poor soul."

"Why 'poor soul'? He chose to go there, so why feel sorry for him?"

"Chose to go? Who did?"

"Who did? Why, he did. Mr. Koga suddenly took it into his head to go, didn't he?"

"Ah. That, you see, is where you're very much mistaken. That's a different kettle of fish."

"Is it? But I just heard it from Redshirt. I don't know about fish, but if I am mistaken, Redshirt's the mother and father of all cock-and-bull stories."

"That's what you'd expect him to say. But you'd also expect Mr. Koga to say that he didn't want to go."

"So they're both right. That's what I like about you, you're always fair. But, tell me, what on earth's it all about?"

"Mr. Koga's mother came this morning and told me all about it."

"What did she say?"

"She said that after Mr. Koga's father died, they hadn't been as well-off as we'd supposed. In fact they were in difficulties. Mrs. Koga went to see the headmaster and asked him if he couldn't pay her son a little more each month, because he'd been at the school for four years."

"I see."

"The headmaster said he would give it serious consideration. Mr. Koga's mother was relieved; she thought they

117

were going to get the first increase they'd had in ages and she kept wondering if it would be this month or next month. Then suddenly the headmaster asked Mr. Koga to go and see him. When he went, the headmaster told him that he was sorry, but the school was short of money and they couldn't raise his salary. He'd heard, however, that there was an opening in Nobeoka and that, since the salary was five yen higher there and he'd thought that it would be what Mr. Koga wanted, he'd already completed all the formalities and Mr. Koga was free to go."

"Then he didn't discuss it with him—he ordered him to go!"

"That's right. Mr. Koga said that he'd rather remain where he was than go somewhere else for more money. He said he had his house and his mother to think of, so could he stay? But the headmaster said it was too late, because when he'd made the arrangements, he'd also found a replacement for Mr. Koga."

"Did he? That's a lousy thing to do—to make a fool of someone. So Mr. Koga doesn't want to go then? I thought it was funny somehow. I mean, no one would be fathead enough to go and live with a lot of monkeys in a place like that, stuck away in the mountains, just for the sake of five yen."

"What does 'fathead' mean?"

"It doesn't matter. Those are just the kind of tactics Redshirt would use. What a rotten thing to do! It's hitting below the belt. And he has the unmitigated gall to say he'll raise my salary. He can say what he likes, I won't let him raise it."

"Are they going to give you a raise?"

"That's what they say, but I'm thinking of refusing."

"Why are you going to refuse?"

"Because I am. Mark my words, that Redshirt's a fool and a sneak."

"A sneak he may be, but if he says he's going to give you

118

a raise, you'd do better to keep quiet and take it. A man often gets angry when he's young, but when he gets older and thinks back, he realizes to his regret that he was a fool not to have been more patient. It stands to reason that you'll kick yourself for being silly. You listen to an old woman: if Redshirt says he's going to give you a raise, say thank you and take it."

"Look, you're an old woman, so mind your own business. It's my salary and I'll decide whether it goes up—or down for that matter."

The old lady left without a word. Old Mr. Hagino was chanting passages of lyrical drama as though he hadn't a care in the world.

It seems to me that this kind of chanting is an art that was deliberately designed to make something which is perfectly understandable when you read it incomprehensible by adding horribly difficult tones. I just couldn't understand how the old man could wail that kind of thing every evening without getting tired of it. However, this was no time to be thinking about lyrical drama.

I hadn't particularly wanted my salary raised, but I'd agreed because I didn't like to see spare money go begging. I wasn't cold-blooded enough, though, to take a cut from the salary of a man who was being transferred against his wishes. What did Redshirt and the others think they were playing at, making Koga settle way down there in Nobeoka? There was a famous public official in the ninth century, Sugawara Michizane, who fell into political disfavor and was sent into exile—but only as far as Hakata. Even Kawai Matagoro, the seventeenth-century assassin, found refuge at Sagara. However, be that as it may, I knew that I wouldn't be satisfied until I'd gone to Redshirt and refused his offer.

I put on my duck-cloth *hakama*[4] and went out once more. Standing in the spacious entrance, I called out and Redshirt's young brother came to the door again. When he saw who it was he gave me a look which plainly said, "What, you again?" If I had business with Redshirt, I'd come as many times as I liked. I'd even knock on his door in the middle of the night if necessary. If he thought I was the kind of person to come and pay my respects to the second master, he was very much mistaken. I'd come because I didn't want my salary increased.

The boy told me that his brother had a visitor at the moment. But when I said that I only wanted a few words with him and that the porch would be fine, he went back into the house. Looking down, I saw a flimsy pair of elegantly shaped clogs. From inside the house I heard someone say, "We've as good as won." I realized that the visitor was Yoshikawa. Only the Clown had such a shrill voice and would wear such arty clogs.

A few moments later Redshirt came to the door, carrying a lamp. "Come in. There's only Yoshikawa here."

"No, thank you. Here will do very well. It won't take long to say what I have to."

Redshirt's round face was flushed as red as a beet. It looked as though he'd been having a few drinks with old Yoshikawa.

"There was some talk, when I was here before, of raising my salary. Well, I've thought it over and changed my mind. I've come to tell you that I don't want to have it increased."

Redshirt held the lamp forward and peered at my face from behind it. The abruptness of my remark had taken him by surprise. He just stood there gaping at me, not knowing what to say. Perhaps he was dumbfounded on being suddenly confronted by the only man in the world to refuse an increase in salary. Or maybe he thought that even if I was going to refuse, there was no need for me to have come back so soon after I'd left. Perhaps it was a combination of both facts that had rooted him where he stood, with his mouth working in a strange way.

"I only accepted before because you told me that Koga was being transferred at his own request, but . . ."

"That's right. Being transferred is partly his own wish."

"No it isn't. He wants to stay here. He wants to stay here where he was born even if it means keeping the same salary."

"Did you hear that from Koga himself?"

"Well, no, not exactly."

"Then who did you hear it from?"

"My landlady heard it from Mr. Koga's mother and told me today."

"So the old lady at your lodgings told you?"

"Well, yes."

"I don't wish to be rude, but that's not quite correct. According to what you say, it sounds as though you believe what the old lady at your lodgings tells you, but not what the second master tells you. Have I understood your meaning correctly?"

I was in a dilemma. BA's are clever devils. They pounce on some nicety and stick with it until they have made their point by worrying and nagging at you. My father often used to say that I was too hasty and harum-scarum. It looked as though he was right. When Mrs. Hagino told me about Koga, I had rushed out impulsively without bothering to find out the details from Koga himself or his mother. Now I was in a predicament. Redshirt had caught me with one of his scholar's thrusts, and I was rather at a loss as to how to parry it.

It was, as I say, difficult to parry this frontal attack, but I'd already marked Redshirt down in my mind as someone not to be trusted. My landlady was, admittedly, tightfisted and grasping, but she wasn't a liar; nor was she two-faced like Redshirt. The only answer I could give was: "What you say may be true, but I still don't wish to have my salary raised."

"Stranger and stranger. As I understand it, you came

here because you had found a reason that made it impossible for you to accept a raise in salary. Yet when I explain things to you and remove that reason, you still decline the increase. I find that a little difficult to understand."

"Difficult to understand or not, I still refuse."

"If you feel so strongly about it, I won't urge you to accept, but you realize that changing fronts as you have within the short space of two or three hours, and without any real reason at that, may affect our faith in you in the future."

"I don't care about that."

"Oh come now! There's nothing more important to a man than trust. Let us just suppose that what your landlord . . ."

"It wasn't the landlord, it was the landlady."

"Well, whoever it was. Let's suppose that what your landlady told you was correct. Your accepting a raise still wouldn't be taking anything away from Koga. He's going to Nobeoka, and a replacement is coming here. That replacement has agreed to teach for rather less than Koga was being paid and we decided to pay you the difference, so there's no need to feel sorry for anybody. Going to Nobeoka is a promotion for Koga, and his replacement agreed from the first to come for less money—which means an increase in salary for you. It couldn't be better for all concerned. Of course you don't have to accept. But why don't you go home and think it over carefully again?"

I'm not very bright, and normally when someone argues as eloquently as Redshirt had, I become convinced that I'm in the wrong and withdraw in confusion. But not tonight. I'd had an aversion to Redshirt right from the outset. It's true that at one time I'd changed my opinion and thought him a kind, rather effeminate sort of man. When I found, however, that he was anything but kind, reaction set in and I began to dislike him more than ever. Thus, no matter how logically and ably he might press his

122

point, however much he might stand on his dignity as second master and try to corner me with words, his arguments made no impression on me.

Just because a man is good at arguing, it doesn't necessarily mean that he's a good person. Nor is it necessarily true that a person who is bested in arguments is bad. On the face of it, Redshirt's arguments were one hundred percent correct, but appearances alone, however attractive, cannot make you fall in love with a person's whole character. If you could buy people's admiration with money, power, or logic, then usurers, policemen, and university professors would have more admirers than anybody else. The idea that I could be won over by the reasoning of a mere middle-school second master was absurd. People work on likes and dislikes, not on reasoning.

"You're perfectly right in what you say, but as I don't want a raise, I—well, I refuse it. There's no point in thinking it over; the answer would still be the same. Goodbye."

With that, I walked out of the gate. Overhead the Milky Way bridged the sky.

9

When I went to school on the morning of the day of Koga's farewell party, Hotta suddenly made the following long-winded apology.

"The other day when Ikagin came and asked me to get you to leave his place because you were too rowdy, I thought he was telling the truth. That's why I asked you to get out. But since then I've found out that he's a bad lot. They say he often sells paintings and drawings with forged signatures and seals, so I'm sure he was lying when he told me about you. He hoped to make some money by selling you some scroll-paintings and antiques, but since you wouldn't have anything to do with him, he made up that pack of lies. I'm very sorry for what I said to you, but I didn't know what kind of a person he was. I hope you'll accept my apology."

I picked up the one and a half *sen* from Hotta's desk without a word and put it in my purse.

"Are you really going to take that back?" Hotta asked incredulously.

"Yes. You see," I explained, "I didn't want to be treated by you, so I was determined to pay you back. But, thinking it over, I gradually came to the conclusion that it would be better if I accepted, so I'm taking the money back."

Hotta let out a great bellow of laughter and said, "Why didn't you take it back sooner?"

"Well, as a matter of fact, I was going to several times, but something always prevented me and I left it there. Every time I've come to school lately it's been a misery to see it."

"You don't like to admit defeat, do you?" remarked Hotta, so I said that he was pretty pigheaded too. After that, something like the following dialogue ensued.

"Where are you from?"

"Tokyo. You?"

"Aizu."

"All people from Aizu are the same: they're all obstinate. Going to the farewell party this evening?"

"Of course. You?"

"Of course I'm going. I was even thinking of going down to the boat to see Koga off."

"Farewell parties are good fun. You wait and see. I'm going to really drink tonight."

"Please yourself. I'm going home as soon as the food's finished. Only fools drink."

"You're always trying to start a fight. You're a typical Tokyoite—flippant and excitable."

"Well, let it drop. Call in at my lodgings on the way to the party, will you? I've got something to tell you."

Hotta came to my lodgings as arranged. Every time I'd seen Koga recently, I'd felt sorry for him, and now, today, when he was going to leave at last, I felt such a great sense of pity for him that, had it been possible, I'd have liked to go in his place. I wanted to make a long speech at the farewell party and give him a hearty send-off, but I knew it was out of the question because of my crude Tokyo language. That's why I'd sent for Hotta. I thought he, with his loud voice, would best be able to frighten the life out of Redshirt.

I started off by telling Hotta about the business with the Madonna, but he knew more about it than I did. I went on to tell him about what had happened by the Nozeri river and called Redshirt a fool. Hotta replied that I was always branding people fools. He said I had called *him* a a fool that day at school. And if he was a fool, Redshirt wasn't, he insisted, because he and Redshirt were out of different molds. Well then, I amended, if Redshirt wasn't a fool he was a shiftless, good-for-nothing dimwit. Hotta readily agreed with this. There was no doubt that Hotta was strong, but it didn't seem that his vocabulary in such matters was a patch on mine. I think all Aizu people are like that.

Next I told Hotta what Redshirt had said about giving me a raise and a more responsible position. At this, he snorted and said it looked as though they were trying to get rid of him. When I asked him if he had any intention of going, he threw out his chest and said that he emphatically had not, and that if he went he'd take Redshirt with him. However, when I put the ball back into his court and asked him how he proposed to accomplish this, he replied that he hadn't thought yet. Hotta looked powerful, but he didn't seem to be very strong on brainwork. I told him I'd refused to have my salary increased. He was very pleased and was full of praise for me, saying that I was a real Tokyoite.

I asked Hotta why, if he knew Koga disliked the idea of leaving so much, he hadn't taken steps to try and keep him where he was. He replied that by the time Koga told him, everything had already been arranged. He had, he said, been to discuss the matter with the headmaster twice and Redshirt once, but that nothing had come of it. In his opinion the trouble was that Koga had been too nice about the whole affair. When Redshirt first spoke to him he should either have refused point-blank or got out of it by saying that he would think it over. Instead, he'd been talked into giving his instant consent by Redshirt, with the result that all his mother's crying and Hotta's intercession had not had the slightest effect. This, said Hotta, was extremely unfortunate. I remarked that I thought the whole thing was a scheme of Redshirt's to get the Madonna by sending Koga away.

"Of course it is," said Hotta. "No doubt about it. He

looks as though butter wouldn't melt in his mouth, but he gets up to all sorts of mischief. If anyone accuses him of anything, he always has a plausible excuse ready. The man's as crafty as a wagonload of monkeys. The only way to deal with a person like that is to teach him a lesson by giving him a good hiding." So saying, Hotta rolled up his sleeve to reveal an arm knotted with muscle.

While we were on the subject, I remarked that he seemed to have strong arms and asked him if he did jujitsu. Hotta flexed the muscles in his forearm and told me to squeeze it. I felt it with the tips of my fingers. It was as hard as the pumice stone in a public bath. I was so impressed that I said that with arms like that I expected he could flatten five or six Redshirts at a time. "Of course I could," he answered, and started to straighten and bend his arm, so that his biceps began to jiggle around under the skin. It was an exhilarating experience. Hotta swore that he could break two plaited twists of paper tied around his biceps by bending his arm and flexing his muscles. I said I supposed I could too.

"Never!" said Hotta. "Go on, try it and see."

I decided not to, since it wouldn't have looked good if I'd failed.

"Hotta, how about it? After you've had a good drink at the farewell party tonight, why don't you give Redshirt and the Clown a thrashing?" I suggested half-jokingly. But Hotta thought about it quite seriously and then said he didn't think he would tonight. When I asked why, he answered that it would put Koga in an awkward position and, besides, if he was going to thrash the pair of them, he'd have to do it when he caught them in the act of doing something wrong, otherwise he'd be blamed for it. This sounded sensible to me. It appeared that Hotta had more ideas on the subject than I did.

"Well then, make a speech and say a lot of nice things about Koga. My Tokyo dialect is too fast and smooth; it lacks the proper weight. Not only that; whenever the time comes for me to speak, my mouth fills with bile, a large lump comes into my throat, and no words come out; so I'll leave it to you," I said.

"That's a strange illness. So you can't speak in front of people? That must be inconvenient."

"It's not inconvenient at all," I replied.

Hotta and I talked until it was time to go to the party and then left together.

The party was to be held at a place called the Kashintei. This was supposed to be the finest restaurant in the area, but I'd never been there before. I'd heard that the building had originally been the mansion of the chief retainer of the local lord and had been purchased and opened as a restaurant just as it was. The place did, in fact, have an imposing appearance. Turning the mansion of a chief retainer into a restaurant is like turning a military coat into underwear.

Most of the others were already present when Hotta and I arrived. They stood around in two or three groups in a large room about thirty feet by thirty. The *tokonoma* was as wonderfully large as you would expect in a room of that size. I'd thought the *tokonoma* large in the fifteen-by-eighteen room I'd occupied at the Yamashiroya, but there was no comparison with this one. It measured twelve feet in width. In the alcove on the right stood a *setomono* vase with a red pattern. In it was a large pine branch. I wondered what the idea of the pine branch was and then concluded that it was to save money, since, unlike flowers, pine would last month after month.

I asked the natural history teacher where the *setomono* vase had been made, only to be told that it wasn't *setomono* but Imari-ware. I said that I thought Imari-ware was *setomono*, at which he just laughed. I found out later that they only use the word *setomono* for earthenware that is made in Seto. Coming from Tokyo, I'd thought the word applied to any earthenware.

128

In the center of the alcove hung a large scroll. On it were twenty-eight Chinese characters, each about the size of my face. They looked badly written to me. They looked so bad, in fact, that I asked the teacher of Chinese classics why they'd hung such a thing so conspicuously. He told me that the characters had been written by the famous calligrapher, Nukina Kaioku, who lived at the turn of the nineteenth century. Kaioku or not, I still think they were badly written.

Eventually Kawamura, the secretary, told us all to be seated, and I found a place near a pillar that I could lean back against. The Badger, as the most important person present, sat in front of the Kaioku scroll. He was dressed in formal *haori*[5] and *hakama*. Redshirt, also in the same attire, had taken up his place on the Badger's left. Koga, as the evening's guest of honor, sat on the Badger's right. He too wore Japanese dress. The Western clothes that I was wearing made it too uncomfortable to kneel formally and I immediately sat cross-legged. The sports master next to me, however, despite his black trousers, was keeping himself in training by sitting with his legs folded under him in the formal kneeling position. Eventually the food arrived on individual, portable tables. On each there stood a flask of *sake*.

The teacher who had made the arrangements for the party stood up and opened the proceedings. He was followed by the Badger, and then by Redshirt. They all, in their farewell speeches to Koga, were unanimous in announcing what an excellent teacher and a fine man he was, and how his leaving was not only a sad loss to the school but a matter of regret to them as individuals also. They all maintained, however, that since the transfer was the earnest wish of Mr. Koga himself, they must reluctantly allow him to go. They weren't in the least embarrassed at throwing a farewell party for Koga and telling such a pack of lies. Of the three of them, Redshirt was the most profuse in his praise of Koga. He expressed sadness at loosing such a good friend. Strangely enough, he sounded as though he meant what he was saying. He spoke, as always, in a quiet, gentle voice, and I knew that anybody hearing him for the first time would be convinced of his sincerity. In all probability he'd caught the Madonna by the same trick. Right in the middle of Redshirt's speech, Hotta, who was sitting opposite me, telegraphed what he thought of Redshirt with a flash of his eyes. I signaled my agreement by pulling my lower eyelid down with my index finger.

No sooner had Redshirt sat down than Hotta leaped to his feet. I was so pleased at this that I found myself applauding. I was a little embarrassed when everyone from the Badger down turned and looked at me, but I was all ears to hear what Hotta was going to say.

"The headmaster and second master have just said how unfortunate it is that Mr. Koga is being transferred. I'm afraid I don't quite agree. I earnestly hope that Mr. Koga will leave this place without delay. I know that Nobeoka is a remote, out-of-the-way place, and that it may have some material disadvantages compared with here. But I have heard that it is a pastoral spot, where manners and customs are of the simplest and where both teachers and pupils alike are gentle and well-behaved, like the people of past ages. There are, I believe, no fops there who go around dispensing flattery they do not really mean and using their outward charm to trap a gentleman. I am sure, therefore, that a kind and sincere person like yourself, Mr. Koga, will be warmly welcomed by everyone there, and I wish to congratulate you heartily on your transfer.

"In conclusion, let me just say that when you arrive in Nobeoka, I hope you will find a wonderful woman, fit to be the wife of a gentleman, and build a happy and peaceful family life for yourself as soon as possible—thereby, in effect, causing a certain faithless hussy to die of shame."

Hotta loudly cleared his throat twice and sat down.

I thought about clapping again, but stopped myself because I didn't want everyone to look at me. After Hotta sat down, Koga got to his feet. Instead of speaking from where he was, he politely walked to the side of the room and, with a low bow to everyone, made the following speech:

"I have recently decided to move to Kyushu for personal reasons and I would like to say how deeply touched I am, gentlemen, that you should have given me this truly magnificent farewell party. I shall never forget it. I am particularly grateful for the kind things said about me by the headmaster and the second master and the other gentlemen; and I would like you to know that those words will always remain with me. Although I shall be far away, I hope that you won't forget me, but will remember me with the kindness you have always shown me." Koga bowed low again—virtually prostrating himself, and then returned to his place.

Koga's goodness was almost unlimited. There he was, respectfully thanking the headmaster and Redshirt—the very people who were making such a fool of him. It wasn't just for the sake of formality, either; you could tell from his manner, his way of speaking and his face that he was really and truly grateful. You would have thought that when the Badger and Redshirt heard themselves being thanked in all good faith by a saint like Koga, they would have had the grace to feel some compassion for him and blushed; but they both sat there and accepted his thanks seriously.

As soon as the speeches were finished, the sound of sucking and slurping arose on all sides. I followed suit and tried some of the soup, but it was dreadful. Some hashed fish had been served with the soup. It was so dark that I thought they must have bought the cheapest kind of fish and then made a mess of preparing it. There was also a dish of sliced raw fish. Instead of being cut finely, however, it was in great slabs. It was like eating raw tuna steaks. Nevertheless, the people around me seemed to be enjoying the food. They'd probably never tasted Tokyo cooking.

It wasn't long before hot flasks of *sake* started to circulate freely, and suddenly the whole place burst into life. The Clown knelt in front of the headmaster and, according to custom, asked him for his *sake* cup so that he could drink his health. Disgusting! Koga was going the rounds, exchanging drinks with people. It looked as though he intended to do it with everyone. What a job! When he came to me, he knelt and, arranging the folds of his *hakama* correctly, asked me for my cup. I sat up in the formal position, although it was uncomfortable in my trousers, and poured him a drink.

"What a pity we have to say goodbye so soon," I said. "We've only just met. When do you leave? I'll come down to the beach to see you off."

"Oh, no! You're far too busy. You mustn't go to all that trouble," Koga replied.

Whatever Koga said, however, I still intended to take some time off from school and go to see him off.

Within the next hour the place really became disorderly. One or two were speaking thickly, slurring their words, and you could hear such snatches of conversation as, "Have a drink—Hey! Have a drink, I said." I was a little bored and went outside to the lavatory. I was standing staring at the old-style garden in the starlight when Hotta came out.

"Well, what did you think of my speech? Good, eh?" He seemed elated. I told him that I agreed with everything he'd said in general, but that there was one place I didn't like.

"Where was that?" he asked.

"You said that there were no fops in Nobeoka who would try to trap a man with their outward charm, didn't you?"

"Yes."

"Well, 'fops' wasn't enough."

"Oh? What should I have said?"

"You should have said: foppish, swindling, mounte-bank, wolf-in-sheep's-clothing, cheating-tinker, fly-by-night, dirty, spying, if-they-barked-you-couldn't-tell-'em-from-a-dog—rogues."

"I couldn't get my tongue round all that. You're very fluent. And anyway, for one thing, you know lots of words. I must say, it's funny you can't speak in public."

"Oh, they're just the stock words I filed away for when I have a quarrel. I can't speak as freely as that when I make a speech."

"No? But, you know, that string of words just rolled out. Say it again."

"As many times as you like. Ready? Foppish, swin-dling, mountebank . . ."

I'd only gone that far, when two people came staggering and clumping along the verandah at a great pace.

"Hey!" they called. "You two! You can't run off like that . . . You can't leave as long as we're here . . . Come and have a drink . . . Mountebank? That's good. Mounte-bank's good . . . Come and have a drink."

So saying, they dragged Hotta and me off with them. As a matter of fact, they'd both probably come out to go to the lavatory, but being drunk they'd forgotten all about it and hauled us off instead. Whenever a drunk sees any-thing happening he always thinks he has to poke his nose in and becomes oblivious to everything that went before.

"Gen'lmen, I've caught a mountebank. Give 'im a drink. Give 'im a lot. Get the mountebank drunk. Hey! You musn' run away."

I hadn't tried to run away, but the drunk pushed me up against the wall. I looked around the room and saw that there wasn't a dish of food that had been left untouched on any of the tables. There were some people even who had finished their own food and advanced ten or twelve yards forward on foraging expeditions. I don't know when the headmaster left, but he was no longer in evidence.

I heard a voice asking if the room was this way, and three or four geisha came in. I was rather surprised, but, being pinned to the wall, I just kept still and looked on. As the girls entered, Redshirt, who up till then had been leaning against a pillar of the *tokonoma* with his amber pipe in his mouth, looking self-satisfied, suddenly got to his feet and started to leave the room. One of the geisha smiled and bowed, and said something as they passed. She was the youngest and prettiest of them. I wasn't close enough to hear what she'd said, but I think it was only something like, "Oh, good evening." Redshirt, ignoring her, left the room and didn't come back. I expect he followed the headmaster and went home.

The room suddenly became cheerful with the arrival of the geisha. The cheers and yells that greeted them from all quarters were so loud that they sounded like war cries. Some began to play odds-and-evens with the geisha. The yells they gave as they played reminded me of the cries that swordsmen give when they practice the quick-draw from a kneeling position.

Others, near me, were engrossed in a complicated game of "stone, scissors, paper," waving both hands about and interspersing shouts of "Yo!" and "Ha!" as they played. Their jigglings and gesticulations were a lot better than those dolls in Dark's puppet theater.[6]

In the far corner one man was shouting for a geisha to pour him a drink; then, realizing that his flask was empty, he waved it in the air and changed his appeal to one for more *sake*. The place was unbearably noisy and rowdy. The only man in the room who didn't know what to do with himself was Koga. He sat there with his head bent, lost in thought. They hadn't thrown this farewell party for his sake, nor because they were sorry that he was being transferred. It was so they could all drink and enjoy themselves,

One of the geisha smiled and bowed, and said something as they passed.

and so he could sit there by himself, twiddling his thumbs. It would have been a lot better to have had no party at all than one like this.

After a while the room was filled with a cacophony as each person began to sing his own particular song in a thick, raucous voice. A geisha came and sat in front of me and asked me to sing something, holding her *samisen* ready to accompany me. I replied brusquely that I didn't sing, but told her to. She began singing:

> *If they walk the streets with drum and gong,*
> *With a tom tom tom, and a ching ching ching,*
> *And find a child who is lost,*
> *With a tom tom tom, and a ching ching ching;*
> *Then beat the drum and ring the gong,*
> *With a tom tom tom, and a ching ching ching,*
> *For there's a man I too would find,*
> *With a tom tom tom, and a ching ching ching.*

She sang the whole song in two breaths and then said, "Whew! That's tiring."

Why hadn't she sung something easier if that one was going to make her puff?

Yoshikawa had appeared from somewhere and sat beside her.

"Poor Suzu. The man you wanted to meet left just when you thought you'd found him," he said, sounding as usual like a professional storyteller. The girl tossed her head and said she didn't know what he was talking about. But the Clown, taking no notice, continued by trying to sing a snatch from the ballad drama *Asagao Nikki*, which tells the pathetic love story of a blind girl. *"By chance I met him; ah! but then . . ."* He had a terrible voice. The geisha told him to stop and gave him a slap on the knee. Yoshikawa was immensely pleased by this and his face split in a grin. This was the geisha who had said good evening to Redshirt. Apparently the Clown wasn't averse to a playful slap from a geisha either.

"Suzu," he said, "I'm going to dance. Play *Kiinokuni* for me."

"Good grief!" I thought. "Is he going to dance too?"

The old teacher of Chinese classics sitting across the way began to sing, contorting his toothless mouth this way and that and trying to imitate a woman's voice: "*Ah, Gembei. How could you be so cruel? After all we've meant to each other . . .*" He got that far safely, but asked a geisha, "What comes next?" Old men have shocking memories.

One of the geisha had buttonholed the natural history teacher and was asking him if he'd like to hear a song that had just come out.

"Now pay attention and listen," she said and began to sing about a modern girl whose hair was dressed in foreign style and tied up with a white ribbon; who rode a bicycle, played the violin, and who only knew a smattering of English, but went around saying to everyone, "I am glad to see you." The natural history teacher was impressed and thought the song amusing because it had some English in it.

Hotta called out in a tremendous voice, "Geisha! geisha! I'm going to do a sword dance. Play the *samisen*."

His tone was so violent that the geisha just stared at him in amazement and didn't answer. Not to be put off by details, Hotta advanced alone into the middle of the floor, carrying a walking stick to serve as a sword; and with the song "*The wreaths of cloud round myriad lofty peaks crushed beneath my feet . . .*" he performed his party piece.

The Clown had exhausted his repertoire of dances, having been through *Kiinokuni*, *Kappore* and *The Daruma on the Shelf*, and now began to march up and down the room, naked except for a loincloth and singing the war song which begins with the words, "*Negotiations between Japan and China have been broken off.*" Lunatic!

I felt sorry for Koga, who had been sitting there all the time looking uncomfortable and still wearing his *hakama*.

Even if it was his own farewell party, I thought, there was no need for him to put up with watching a near-naked dance by a madman in a loincloth, while *he* was in full Japanese dress. I went over to him and suggested that we leave.

"This is my farewell party and it would be rude if I left first, but you go ahead, please," he answered, and refused to budge.

"Don't worry about that. If it's a farewell party they should behave as though it was. Look at them all! This isn't a farewell party, it's a madhouse. Let's go."

I persisted, and at last Koga rose to follow me. But as we were about to leave the room, the Clown came up wielding a broom and exclaiming, "Good gracious! We can't have the guest of honor going home first! We're having Sino-Japanese negotiations. I won't let you pass!" So saying, he held the broom crosswise and blocked our path.

All my pent-up anger boiled to the surface and I said, "Well, if these are Sino-Japanese relations, you must be a Chink." With this, I gave him a smart rap on the head with my fist.

For two or three seconds he just stood there gawping like a gaffed fish. Then, finding his voice, he came out with a meaningless stream of words.

"How dreadful! Ah, cruel blow! You struck me! Me, Yoshikawa! Many thanks. This has really turned into Sino-Japanese negotiations."

While he was in full spate, Hotta, noticing the excitement, stopped his sword dance and came bounding up from behind Yoshikawa. Seeing how things stood, he shot out his hand, grabbed the Clown by the scruff of the neck and yanked him backwards.

"Sino-Japanese . . . Ouch! Ouch! This is violence!" He was twisting this way and that in an effort to escape, when Hotta flipped him sideways and he landed on the floor with a thud.

I don't know what happened after that. Koga and I parted on our way home, and I arrived back at my lodgings just after eleven o'clock.

10

The school had a holiday to celebrate the victory of the Japanese army in China. There was to be a ceremony on the town parade ground, and the Badger had to attend at the head of the pupils. As a member of the staff, I had to go too. The whole town was so ablaze with the Japanese sun flag that it was dazzling.

There were eight hundred pupils in the school. The plan was for the sports master to dress the ranks, and for the whole school to march in companies, with one or two teachers in the space between each company to keep control. That was the plan. On paper it was the picture of ingenuity, but when put into effect, it produced something that was extraordinarily clumsy.

Since the boys were not only childish but impertinent too, and thought that it reflected on their good name if they didn't break the rules, it served no useful purpose to have teachers with them, however many there were. They sang war songs, without waiting for instructions, and when they'd finished singing let out great whoops and yells. All in all, it was as though a band of lawless samurai were tramping through the streets.

When they weren't singing war songs or yelling, they were chattering among themselves. You'd think that it would have been possible to walk without chattering, but all Japanese are born into the world mouth first, and no amount of scolding would stop the boys. Plain chattering wouldn't have been too bad, but this vulgar crew were saying insulting things about the teachers. I'd thought I'd taught the boys a lesson when I'd made them apologize for what had happened when I was on night duty, but that was a big mistake. To borrow a phrase from my landlady, getting them to apologize was one thing, but teaching them a lesson was altogether a "different kettle of fish."

When the boys had apologized, it hadn't been because they were truly sorry for what they'd done. Their apology had been a mere formality—something that they had done because the headmaster had ordered them to.

In the same way that a merchant will bow and scrape and continue to cheat you, the general run of pupils will apologize without the least idea of giving up mischief. On reflection, it seems that the world is composed entirely of people like those boys. People apologize to you and say they're sorry, but they think you're a fool and too naive if you take their apology seriously and are willing to forgive them. You won't go far wrong if you remember that when somebody apologizes to you, he doesn't really mean it, and therefore you should only pretend to forgive him. The only way to make someone really apologize is to beat him until he truly regrets what he's done.

As I was marching along between two of the companies, I heard the words "fried prawns" and "dumplings" time and again. There were too many boys to know who was saying it. Even if I'd been able to find out the culprits, they were bound to deny that they'd been talking about me and would have said that it was nervous debility that made me suspect they had been. Such cowardice was a habit, having been nurtured in the area from feudal times, and I was afraid that even I, for all my integrity, would begin to copy it if I remained in the place for a year.

I wasn't so stupid as to let the boys talk themselves out of a situation in such a way that I was made to look a fool and put in the wrong. Two could play at that game. Pupils or not—children or not—they were bigger than I was, and in common justice I was entitled to retaliate and punish them. The only problem was, however, that if I tried to

141

retaliate in some ordinary way, they would turn the tables on me. If I accused them of anything, they'd effusively insist on their innocence with all sorts of excuses that they'd prepared beforehand. Having argued eloquently and put themselves apparently in the right, they'd turn and attack me. Since my object was retaliation, I could not vindicate myself unless I brought their wrong to light. In short, if I couldn't do so, people would think that I was the real cause of the quarrel even though the boys had instigated it; and if that happened, it would be a calamity for me. On the other hand, if I was lazy and let them get away with it, they'd be more puffed-up than ever and that, to exaggerate but a little, wouldn't be a good thing for the world at large. It seemed that the only way open to me was to take a leaf out of their book and retaliate in such a manner that they couldn't pin anything on me; but that would degrade me, a Tokyoite, too. But, degrading or not, I am only human, and I knew that if I stayed in the place for a year, being constantly bested by the boys, I'd do it, because there would be no other way to settle things with them. The only thing for me to do was to return to Tokyo and Kiyo as quickly as possible. It was as though living in the country spelled degeneration for me. I'd have been better delivering papers for a living than to have sunk to this.

I was walking reluctantly along with the boys, mulling all this over in my mind, when suddenly I heard a commotion coming from up front. At the same time, the column came to a full stop. I thought this was odd and moved right, out of the line, to take a look. The corner where Yakushimachi branches off from Ōtemachi was completely congested and a confused mass of people was jostling, pushing forward and being pushed back. The sports master came down the line, shouting in a hoarse voice for everyone to quiet down. I asked him what was happening, and he replied that our middle school and the normal school had clashed at the corner.

I've heard that a middle school and a normal school in any prefecture are like cat and dog. Why, I don't know, but it seems that their characters are so radically different that they just can't get along together. They fight on the slightest pretext. I imagined that for these boys living a restricted life in the country this was just a way of killing time.

I'm rather partial to a fight, so, partly out of curiosity, I ran towards the head of the column when I heard that there had been a clash. Some of our boys up front were yelling for the normal school to get back and shouting, "Get out of the way! You've only got a school because of the local taxpayers!" Others behind them were calling out, "Push! Push!"

I was elbowing through the boys who were blocking the way and had nearly reached the corner, when I heard the command, "Forward march!" given in a high, sharp voice. At this, the normal school started to move forward quietly. Some agreement had clearly been reached about the original bone of contention. Our school, in fact, had given ground. The normal school is said to have a higher standard than the middle school.

The victory celebration ceremony was very simple. A brigadier from the army read a congratulatory address and the prefectural governor read another. Everyone on the parade ground gave three cheers and that was the end.

I'd heard that there was to be some entertainment, but not until the afternoon, so I went back to my lodgings for a while and began to write to Kiyo, because it had been on my mind for some time. Kiyo had asked me for a longer letter with more details than I'd written before, and I felt obliged to do as she'd asked as conscientiously as possible. When I actually got some paper and tried to write, however, I had so much to say that I didn't know where to begin. Some things I rejected because they were too troublesome to put down on paper, and others because

143

they weren't interesting. I wondered if there wasn't something that wouldn't be too difficult to write about and yet, at the same time, would be interesting for Kiyo to read. Nothing that had happened to me seemed to fulfill those two requirements. I rubbed my ink-stick on the stone, dipped my brush into the ink and gazed at the paper. I gazed at the paper, dipped my brush into the ink and rubbed my ink-stick on the stone: the same actions over and over again. I finally decided that I couldn't write letters and, giving up the attempt, put the lid back on the ink-box.

Throwing aside my brush and writing paper, I rolled over onto my stomach, pillowed my head on my arm and looked out at the garden. I was anxious about Kiyo, but I felt sure that she would be aware of my concern for her health—that my true feelings would somehow communicate themselves to her. And if that was so, it wasn't necessary to send her a letter. If she didn't hear from me she would assume that I was well. You only need to write a letter if someone dies or is ill, or when something happens.

The garden was a plain, flat area about forty yards square, without any kind of rockery or other relief, and with no flowers or plants to speak of. There was, however, an orange tree which rose high enough above the wall to act as a landmark from outside. Whenever I came home, I would always sit and gaze at this tree. For someone who had never been out of Tokyo before, it was a novelty to see an orange tree with the fruit hanging on the branches. Those green oranges would gradually ripen and turn yellow. They would, I thought, look pretty. There were already some whose color had partly changed. When I asked my landlady about the oranges, she said they were very juicy and sweet. She told me that they would soon be ripe and that when they were I could eat as many as I liked. I'd made up my mind to eat two or three every day. I thought they'd be ready for eating in another three weeks at the most. I couldn't see the faintest possibility of my

144

leaving there before that time. While I was thinking about the oranges, Hotta happened to drop by to talk to me.

"As today's a victory celebration," he said, "I bought some beef so that you and I could have a good feed together."

He slipped a package wrapped in a bamboo sheath from the sleeve of his kimono and tossed it into the middle of the room. Not only had I been subjected to torture by potatoes and bean-curd in my lodgings, I was also under an interdict not to go to a noodle or a dumpling shop. I told Hotta that the meat was a wonderful idea, went and borrowed a pan and some sugar from old Mrs. Hagino at once, and set about cooking it.

Cramming beef into his mouth, Hotta asked me whether I knew that Redshirt had a regular geisha.

"Of course I knew," I answered. "She was one of the girls that came to Koga's farewell party the other evening, wasn't she?"

"That's right. I only just realized it. You're very shrewd." After this compliment Hotta continued, "He's forever talking about 'character' and 'spiritual recreation' and all the time the cheeky devil's having an affair with a geisha on the sly. It'd be all right if he was tolerant of other people enjoying themselves, but he isn't. I mean, it was Redshirt who warned you, through the headmaster, that just going to a noodle or a dumpling shop would be bad for discipline, wasn't it?"

"Yes. He seems to think that buying himself a geisha is spiritual recreation, but that eating fried prawns or dumplings is material pleasure. If that's spiritual recreation why doesn't he do it openly? What does he think he's playing at? When his favorite geisha came into the room, he stood up and slipped away. I can't stomach him, because he's always trying to fool people. If you attack him, he'll try and pull the wool over your eyes by saying he doesn't know what you mean, or by talking about Russian literature, or

145

saying that modern poetry is the bosom friend of the *haiku*. A weakling like that isn't a man! He's like a reincarnation of a court lady-in-waiting. Perhaps his father was one of the 'backroom boys' at the famous teahouse in front of the Michizane shrine at Yushima."

"What were they?"

"Well, whatever they were, they weren't exactly masculine . . . That part's not cooked yet. You'll get a tapeworm if you eat it like that."

"Oh? I think it's about done, though. Anyway, they say Redshirt goes into the hot-spring town without anyone knowing and meets his geisha at the Kadoya."

"Kadoya? Is that that inn?"

"It's an inn and a restaurant. I'm going to keep watch and catch him red-handed going in with the girl. Then I'll confront him with it on the spot. That's the best way to get Redshirt."

"Keep watch? You mean, all night?"

"Yes. There's an inn called Masuya on the opposite side of the road to the Kadoya, right? I'll take a room on the second floor at the front, poke a hole in one of the paper screens overlooking the street and keep watch through that."

"Do you think he'll come while you're watching?"

"I should think so. One night won't be any good. I'll have to be prepared to do it for two weeks."

"You'll do yourself some harm, you know. I sat up for a week nursing my father just before he died. Afterwards I felt listless and as weak as a kitten."

"I don't mind if it does affect me a little. It'd be a disservice to Japan to let a rogue like him carry on that way, so I'm going to execute him in the name of Heaven."

"Excellent! If that's what you've decided to do, I'll join you. Shall we start keeping watch tonight?"

"No, we can't tonight. I haven't spoken to them at the Masuya yet."

146

"Well, when do you intend to start?"

"Soon. I'll let you know when, and then you can come and help me."

"Good. I'll help you any time. I'm no good at planning things, but I'm pretty nimble in a fight."

As Hotta and I were eagerly discussing our plan for a crusade against Redshirt, my landlady came and said that one of the pupils had called to see Hotta. He had, it seemed, gone to Hotta's place, but, finding him out, had come here because this was where he had thought he'd probably be. Having delivered her message, Mrs. Hagino waited, kneeling on the threshold, for Hotta's reply.

"I see," said Hotta, and walked out to the front porch.

He returned after a while and said to me, "The boy came to ask me if I'd like to go and see the sideshows and the entertainment they're having as part of the victory celebrations. Apparently there's a large troupe of dancers who've come all the way from Kōchi to do some dance or other. He says I shouldn't miss it, as it's not often that you get a chance to see it. You come and see it with me."

Hotta was very eager for me to go. I'd seen any number of dances in Tokyo. Every year at the festival of the Hachimon shrine they used to pull a movable stage through the streets, so I knew *Shiokumi* and all the other dances. I had no wish to see some meaningless dance from Tosa. Hotta's taking the trouble to ask me, however, made me feel somehow that I'd like to go, and we walked out of the gate together. The boy who had come to call for Hotta was Redshirt's young brother. There was something fishy about that.

Around the grounds where the entertainment was to be held were a number of flagpoles from which flew long pennants. The scene reminded me of the Ekōin temple when they have a wrestling tournament, or the Honmonji temple when they hold a Buddhist mass. Besides the pennants, the place was festooned with string upon string of

147

flags, as though they'd borrowed a flag from every country in the world. The broad expanse of the sky had been changed into a gay tapestry by these decorations. In the eastern corner of the grounds stood a hastily erected stage on which the something-or-other dance from Kōchi was to be performed.

About fifty yards or so to the right of the stage there was a booth made of rush-blinds where they were displaying examples of the art of flower-arranging. Everyone was gazing at the arrangements with admiration, but I thought they were all so much rubbish. A person who enjoys looking at twisted plants or bamboo might just as well be proud of having a hunchbacked lover or a lame husband.

On the side of the grounds away from the stage, fireworks were being set off and rockets were rising thick and fast into the air. One of the rockets released a balloon on which was written *Long Live the Empire*. It drifted over the pine trees around the castle keep and came to earth in the barracks. Bang! Another rocket rose like a black dumpling, hissing into the air and seeming to cleave through the autumn sky. When it was directly over my head it burst, and streamers of green smoke arched out like the ribs of an umbrella and were then swept away into the depths. Another balloon went up. This one had *Long Live the Army and the Navy* written in white on a red ground. It was caught by the wind, wafted off over the hot-spring town and then on in the direction of the village of Aioi. Perhaps it finally came to earth there in the compound of the Kannon temple.

There hadn't been many people present at the ceremony in the morning, but now the place was packed. I was surprised to see that so many people lived in a country town like this. The place was swarming. There wasn't much to be seen in the way of intelligent faces, but numerically the crowd wasn't to be laughed at. Soon the troupe from Kōchi that everyone had been talking about began their dance. When I had heard the word "dance" I'd jumped to the conclusion that it would be something like the Fujima school of dancing do. I was very much mistaken.

Three rows, each composed of ten men, extended across the stage. Each man wore an imposing band tied around his head and knotted at the back, and a *hakama* which was girded up around his knees. What really astonished me was that every one of the thirty men carried a drawn sword. The three rows were separated from each other by about eighteen inches and each man had that distance, or perhaps less, between himself and those on either side of him. One man stood alone on the edge of the stage, away from the others. This solitary figure wore a *hakama* like his colleagues, but had dispensed with the headband and, instead of a drawn sword, carried a drum slung across his chest. It was the same kind of drum as they use when they perform a lion dance in the streets.

After a while he chanted, "Iyaa—, Haa—" in a leisurely voice and began to sing a weird song, beating the drum rhythmically as he did so. I'd never heard such a strange melody before. You won't be far out if you imagine it as a cross between the comic song which strolling players sing at New Year and a melancholy hymn. The melody was extremely lethargic and as formless as jelly in midsummer, but the drummer punctuated it with beats on his drum and this served to keep a constant rhythm. The drawn swords flashed in time with this rhythm, and such was the rapidity and skill required, I broke out in a cold sweat, although I was only an onlooker.

Imagine it from the dancers' point of view. Eighteen inches to either side, and behind and in front of you, is a living person who is wielding a sharp, naked blade, the same as you. Unless you keep strictly in time, you'll hit one of your colleagues and someone will get hurt. It wouldn't have been so dangerous if they were only standing still, just swinging the swords before and behind, or up and

149

down; but sometimes all thirty of them would give a stamp and turn to the side; sometimes they would spin in a complete circle, or bend their knees. If the person next to you was a fraction too quick or too slow, you might lose your nose, or split his head open. Each man had complete control of his own sword, but not only was that sword walled in on all sides in an area eighteen inches square, it also had to be brandished in the same direction and at the same speed as those of the people before and behind and to left and right.

I was told that it takes years of devoted practice to perform this dance, and that it's extremely difficult to keep the time. They say the man who has the most difficult job of all is the maestro who puts in those indispensible drum beats. Every movement of the legs and hands and every bend of the hips of thirty men is decided by the rhythm of our friend with the drum. What is surprising is that it looks as though the drummer has the easiest time, and that all he has to do is chant, "Iyaa—, Haa—" in a leisurely way, whereas, in fact, he has a very heavy responsibility and an extraordinarily arduous task.

Hotta and I were filled with admiration and were engrossed in watching the dance when, all of a sudden, a loud yell went up about a hundred yards away and all the people who had up till then been quietly inspecting the various sideshows abruptly began to move in great waves to right and left. "Fight! Fight!" somebody shouted, and all at once Redshirt's young brother threaded his way through the crowd and said, "Sir! They're fighting again. The middle school's going to get its own back for what happened this morning. They're going to fight it out to the finish with the normal school. Come on, sir. Hurry!"

He'd no sooner finished than he slipped back into the waves of people and was gone.

"Are those kids at it again? They're the bane of my life. Can't they ever stop?" said Hotta, and dashed off at full tilt, dodging around the people who were trying to get away. Since he could hardly just stand and watch the fight, I imagined he was going to try and break it up. Needless to say, I had no intention of running away, and set off on Hotta's heels for where the fight was. When I arrived it was in full swing. There were about fifty or sixty pupils from the normal school, but there must have been thirty percent more of our boys. The normal-school boys still wore their uniforms, but the majority of the middle-school pupils had gone home after the ceremony in the morning and changed out of their uniforms into Japanese clothes, thus making it easy to tell who was on who's side. However, they were all mixed up in such a confused melee, now coming together in knots, now disentangling, that I had no idea where to begin in pulling them apart.

Hotta had stood staring in dismay at this chaotic state of affairs for a while, but now he looked across at me and said, "There's nothing for it. There'll be trouble if the police come. We'll have to dive in and break them up." Without any answer, I leaped right into what looked like the thick of the fight.

"Stop it! This violence is a disgrace to your schools. WILL YOU STOP IT!!" I was yelling at the top of my voice and trying to force my way through to what seemed to be the boundary between the opposing armies. Unfortunately it wasn't as easy as all that. Having advanced two or three yards into the crowd, I couldn't go forward and I couldn't retreat.

Just in front of me a comparatively big boy from the normal school was grappling with a fifteen- or sixteen-year-old middle-school boy.

"Stop it! Will you stop it!" I shouted and, grabbing the normal-school boy by the shoulder, tried to pull him off by force. As I did so, someone swept my legs out from under me. Taken by surprise, I released the shoulder I'd been holding and fell sideways. Somebody stood on my back with his hard shoes. I was on my hands and knees and from this position thrust myself upright, sending the boy on my back tumbling off to the right. As I stood up, I caught sight of Hotta about six yards away, his big frame wedged in among the boys, being jostled and shoved back.

"Stop it!" he was shouting. "Stop this fighting!"

"Hey!" I called to him. "It's no good. We're not getting anywhere." But I couldn't make myself heard, and Hotta said nothing.

A stone came whizzing through the air and caught me a smart crack on the cheekbone. At the same time someone behind me started to beat me on the back with a stick. Somewhere I could hear a voice saying, "Teachers! Poking their noses in. Hit 'em! Hit 'em!" Another voice was shouting, "There's two of 'em. A big one and a small one. Stone 'em!"

"What?" I roared. "Less of your lip you cheeky brats. Oafs!" And with this I lashed out and clouted the nearest normal-school boy across the head. Another stone sailed through the air. This one grazed the top of my cropped head and flew off behind me. I couldn't see what had happened to Hotta. There was only one thing for me to do. My original intention had been to stop the fight, but I'd been clubbed and had stones thrown at me. I wasn't about to crawl off with my tail between my legs.

"Who do you think I am?" I shouted again. "I may be small, but Tokyo's the home of fighting, and I can still show you a thing or two."

I flailed about me blindly, hitting people and being hit back, until at last I heard somebody call, "Police! Run for it! It's the police!" Up till then I'd been scarcely able to move and had felt as though I were swimming through dough, but now things seemed to have suddenly become easier. Friend and foe alike had completely disappeared. Oafs and clods they may have been, but they were very adept at retreating. I don't think that even the Russian general Kuropatkin could have made a better retreat from the Japanese army.

I looked round to see what had become of Hotta and saw him standing a little way off, wiping his nose. His unlined *haori* with his family crest on it was in shreds. He'd been hit on the bridge of the nose and had lost a fair amount of blood. His nose was an ugly sight, swollen and bright red. The kimono I was wearing was lined and had a splashed pattern, so, although it was covered with mud, it wasn't in nearly such bad shape as Hotta's *haori*. My cheek, however, stung like anything. Hotta told me that it was bleeding pretty badly.

About fifteen or sixteen policemen had arrived on the scene, but since the boys had all withdrawn in the other direction, Hotta and I were the only ones to get caught. We gave them our names and told them everything that had happened, but they said we had to go to the police station. Having given all the particulars to the chief of police there, I went back to my lodgings.

"

Next morning when I opened my eyes I found that I ached all over. I hadn't had a fight in a long time and was out of training, so I suppose it was only natural that it should have told on me like that. I was lying in bed, thinking that the condition I was in didn't give me much cause to be proud of myself as a fighter, when my landlady brought in the *Shikoku Daily* and put it down near my pillow.

I didn't really even feel in a fit state to read a newspaper, but, thinking that I wouldn't be much of a man if I allowed myself to be beaten by such a trifling matter, I forced myself to roll over onto my stomach and, lying there in bed, I opened the paper at page two.

A shock was in store for me. The previous day's fight had been written up. It wasn't the fact that the story appeared but their account of the fight that gave me a shock. It ran something like this:

Not only did Mr. Hotta (first name unknown), a teacher at the middle school, and a certain insolent Mr. So-and-so, a new teacher from Tokyo, inveigle obedient and law-abiding boys into trouble and instigate a disturbance, they actually took command of the boys present and committed an unprovoked and wanton act of violence against pupils of the normal school. [It went on to say:] *The middle school in this prefecture has always been the envy of the whole country, as a place where a spirit of gentleness and obedience prevailed. Now, through the actions of these two perfidious whelps, the prerogatives of our school have been compromised and the whole town disgraced.*

Under such circumstances we feel obliged to undertake a

vigorous inquiry into where the responsibility lies. We believe,
however, that the authorities concerned will take appropriate
action before we do and ensure that neither of these men can
ever appear in the educational world again.

They'd printed the whole thing in italics in an effort to make the effect more caustic.

"Shit!" I shouted, and leaped out of bed. Before, every joint in my body had been very painful, but as soon as I was up the pain seemed to decrease, oddly enough, and I forgot all about it.

I screwed the newspaper up into a ball and hurled it out into the garden, but this still didn't satisfy me, so I went round and threw it down the toilet.

Newspapers are always telling lies. There isn't anything or anyone in the world more given to exaggeration and making mountains out of molehills than a newspaper. The *Shikoku Daily* had set out in print a lot of things that only I was qualified to comment on. Not only that! What did they mean by "a certain insolent Mr. So-and-so, a new teacher from Tokyo?" Whoever heard of anyone with the name So-and-so? Where was their sense? I have as well-established and decent a name as the next man. If they wanted to see my family tree, I'd show it to them with every one of my ancestors from Tada Mitsunaka down.

When I washed my face, my cheek suddenly started to hurt. Old Mrs. Hagino brought me the mirror I asked for and inquired whether I'd looked at the morning paper. I told her that I'd read it and thrown it down the toilet, and that if she wanted it she could go and fish it out again. She withdrew in surprise. I looked at my face in the mirror and saw that I still had the cut from the previous day. It's not much of a face, but it's important to me. And to have it cut and then, on top of everything else, to be labeled "the insolent Mr. So-and-so" was too much.

Thinking that I'd never live it down if it was said that I'd stayed away from school because I'd been intimidated

155

by the newspaper article, I ate my breakfast quickly and was the first at school. One after another the teachers began to arrive. Every one of them looked at my face and smiled.

"What's so funny?" I thought to myself. "I don't owe you anything for my face—you didn't make it."

After a while Yoshikawa appeared and said, "That was quite an achievement yesterday. Is that the honorable wound?"

I imagined he was getting his own back for my having hit him at the farewell party. He jeered at me so much that I told him to mind his own business and to go and suck his paintbrush.

"I *am* sorry, I'm sure," he replied. "But it must be very painful."

"Painful or not," I roared, "it's my face and I don't need anything from you."

Yoshikawa went and sat at his desk on the other side of the room and whispered something with a grin to the history teacher, sitting next to him.

A little later Hotta put in an appearance. His nose was purple and so swollen that it looked as though pus would gush out if you lanced it. It might have been only vanity on my part, but his face seemed to have fared far worse than mine. Since Hotta's desk and mine were next to each other, it meant that when we sat down we were lined up side by side. To make matters worse, we were unlucky enough to have our desks directly facing the door of the staff room. There they were, those two sorry-looking faces, side by side. I was sure that whenever one of the others got bored with what he was doing he would look across at us. It was also evident that however much they might pretend to sympathize with us, they were really thinking to themselves that we were fools. Otherwise they wouldn't have been whispering together and sniggering as they were.

I was greeted by applause when I went to the classroom, and two or three boys even cheered. But I didn't know whether they meant it or were being sarcastic. Although Hotta and I were the focal point of attention for the whole school, Redshirt alone came up to us as though nothing had happened and remarked that the whole affair was a calamity.

"I feel terribly sorry for you," he said. "But you needn't worry. I've already discussed the article with the headmaster and we've decided to ask them to print a retraction. I feel very badly about the whole thing, because it was my brother that fetched Mr. Hotta. I'm going to make every effort over this business, so I hope you won't hold what has happened against me."

He sounded almost apologetic.

The headmaster came from his room during the third period to see us. He looked very worried and said how embarrassing it was that the newspaper should have written such an article, and that he hoped no complications would arise. I wasn't worried at all, because I'd decided that if they were going to fire me I'd hand in my resignation before they could do so. If I resigned without having done any wrong, however, it would make those loudmouthed newspapermen more presumptuous than ever. By rights, I thought, I should make them print a retraction and carry on teaching at the school, even if I had to dig my heels in to do it. I thought that I might go and talk to them at the newspaper on my way home, but I didn't because Redshirt had said that the school would ask them for a retraction.

When the headmaster and Redshirt had a few minutes to spare, Hotta and I explained to them the truth of the matter. They both accepted our version of the affair and concluded that the newspaper had purposely printed the article because they harbored some grudge against the school.

Redshirt went round to every teacher in the staff room,

defending our action. In particular, he announced that it was his brother that had gone to invite Hotta to the entertainment. The way he spoke made it sound as though he himself had been at fault. Everyone agreed that the newspaper was in the wrong, that it was disgraceful, and that the article was a terrible blow to both Hotta and me.

On our way home Hotta said to me, "You know, there's something fishy about Redshirt. If we're not careful he'll have us."

"There's always been something fishy about him. Today wasn't the first time."

"You don't seem to appreciate it yet, but it was Redshirt's brother that came to call for me at your house, and it was Redshirt's brother that got us involved in the fight."

Hotta was right. I hadn't realized that. I had to admire Hotta; he seemed wild, but he was cleverer than me.

"Redshirt got us into the fight like that, then went straight round to the newspaper office and got them to write that article. The man's a real rogue."

"The article too? Well, I'll be damned! But would the newspaper believe what Redshirt said—just like that?"

"Believe him? There'd be no problem if he had a friend on the paper."

"But does he?"

"Even if he doesn't it'd still be easy. You go to a newspaper, lie to them and tell them such and such happened, and they'll print it straight away."

"That's dreadful! If Redshirt really planned the whole thing we may both lose our jobs over this."

"If things go badly we could find ourselves in trouble."

"In that case I'm going to give my notice in tomorrow and go back to Tokyo. I wouldn't stay in a place like this if they begged me to."

"It won't worry Redshirt if you give your notice."

"That's true. What would worry him?"

"The man's as wily as a fox. He always contrives things

158

so that there's no evidence against him. He's difficult to catch out."

"It's a real problem. If we say anything, we'll be accused of bringing a false charge against him. It's all very discouraging. I sometimes wonder whether there's such a thing as divine justice."

"Anyway, let's see how things go for the next two or three days. Then, if the worst comes to the worst, we'll have to catch him at the hot spring."

"You mean, leave the affair of the fight aside?"

"Yes. We'll take the offensive and hit him where it hurts."

"That's an idea. I'm no good at planning. I'll leave everything to you. But when it comes to the push I'll do anything."

Hotta and I parted at this point. If Hotta's guess about what Redshirt had done was correct, then he really was a rogue. It would be useless to try and beat him in a battle of wits; he was far too clever for us. The only way to beat him was with brute strength. War, I thought, will always be present in the world. Even individuals resort to force to settle things in the end.

The next day I waited impatiently for the newspaper to be delivered. When it eventually came I searched through it, but there was neither correction nor retraction. I went to school and taxed the Badger with this, but he said that it would probably appear the next day. Sure enough, it did; but in small, six-point agate type. It was the correction that the school itself had submitted and there was, of course, no word of apology from the newspaper.

Once again I went to talk the matter over with the headmaster. He said there was nothing more he could do. It seemed that the headmaster really had very little power, for all his badger-like face and his strutting around in a frockcoat. He couldn't even make a country newspaper apologize for writing a libelous article. I was so angry that I told him I would go and talk to the editor myself. But he told me not to, because, if I did, they would only slander me again. He concluded by saying that once a newspaper has written something about you, whether it be true or false, there is nothing you can do about it. One could only resign oneself, he said. He sounded like a priest giving a sermon.

If newspapers are really like that then the sooner they are all smashed and put out of business the better for everybody. The Badger's words made me realize for the first time that a newspaper has a lot in common with a snapping turtle: once either of them latch on to you they won't let go.

About three days later, in the afternoon, Hotta came round in a towering rage to see me. He said that the time was ripe at last, and that he was going to carry out the plan he'd told me about. I immediately replied that, if that was the case, he could count me in. Hotta, however, shook his head and said that I'd better not.

"Why?" I asked.

Hotta's reply was to inquire whether the headmaster had called me and asked for my resignation.

"No," I answered. "Did he ask for yours?"

"Yes. He called me to his room today and said that he was very sorry but, due to circumstances beyond his control, he'd have to ask for my resignation."

"What kind of a trial is that? You know how a badger is supposed to beat its belly like a drum when it's contented? Well, our Badger must have beaten such a tattoo on his that he's addled his brains. You and I went to the victory celebration together, we went to see those dancers from Kōchi doing the sword dance together, and we tried to stop the fight together. If he's going to ask for resignations, then to be fair he should ask for both yours and mine. Why is it that in country schools they have no idea of logic? It really makes me mad."

"Redshirt's at the back of this. The way everything has turned out up till now, he and I could never work together. But he doesn't see any harm in letting you stay here."

"You think I could work with Redshirt? He's got a damned cheek not to see any harm in my staying here!"

"He thinks you're so naive that he can pull the wool over your eyes even if you do stay."

"That's even worse. As if anybody could work with him!"

"There's another reason too. Something came up, and the man who was supposed to take over from Koga hasn't arrived yet. As things stand, if they threw you and me out together there'd be such a gap in the boys' timetable that it would seriously interfere with their classes."

"So they're just going to use me as a stopgap? Damn! If they think I'm going to fall for that one they're mistaken."

Next day I went to school and spoke to the headmaster in his room.

"Why didn't you ask for my resignation?"

"Pardon?" The Badger was astonished.

"It's absurd to think that you can ask for Hotta's and not for mine."

"There were reasons why, for the sake of the school . . ."

"Well those reasons are wrong. If I needn't resign, why should Hotta?"

"I'm afraid I cannot explain things to you; but while I regard Mr. Hotta's leaving as unavoidable, I see no necessity for you to resign."

Badgers are crafty. And the headmaster was well named. He talked in circles and avoided coming to the point, and yet he was completely self-possessed.

I saw no other way out, so I said, "Then I resign too. You may have thought, sir, that I would stand idly by while you dismissed Hotta by himself, but I'm afraid that I can't be so callous."

"You can't do that. If you both leave we shan't be able to teach mathematics at the school at all, and . . ."

"Whether you can or not is nothing to do with me."

"You can't be that selfish. You must have a little consideration for the position the school is in. Another thing: if you resign now, when you haven't been here a month, it will have a serious effect on your future career. That's something you should give some thought to."

"I don't care about my career. Justice is more important to me."

"But of course. What you say is absolutely right. But please try and appreciate what I am saying. If you are determined to resign, then I won't try and stop you. But I would like you to remain until we can find a replacement. Anyway, go home and think it over again."

My reasons for leaving the school were so plain that I knew no amount of reconsideration would make me change my mind. But the Badger's face was paling and flushing by turns, so, feeling sorry for him, I said I would think it over again and left. I didn't say anything about the matter to Redshirt, because I thought that since we were going to settle our account with him anyway, it would be better to do so all at once.

When I told Hotta all that had passed between the Badger and myself, he said that he'd guessed something of the sort would happen, but that it wouldn't interfere with our plans if I were to postpone giving my notice until the the last minute. I did as he said. He seemed to have a better head on his shoulders than me, and I made up my mind to do whatever he advised.

Hotta at last handed in his resignation, said goodbye to the other teachers, and went to the Minatoya, the inn down by the beach. Unbeknown to anyone, however, he doubled back to the Masuya in the hot-spring town and went into hiding in a second-floor room at the front, where he poked a hole in the paper screen and began to keep watch. I was the only one who knew this.

Redshirt could only attempt to go to the inn opposite at night. Early evening would be too dangerous because of the chance of being seen by pupils or other prying eyes. The earliest he would appear would be nine o'clock. For the first two nights I kept watch with Hotta until eleven o'clock, but there was no sign of Redshirt. The third night we watched from nine till half past ten, but still with no luck. There's nothing, I felt, so ridiculous as having to tramp back to your lodgings in the middle of the night after a fruitless watch. After four or five nights of this, my landlady began to feel a little concerned. She said that a married man shouldn't go gadding about at night. I told her that what I was playing at at night wasn't the kind of playing she thought at all—that I was about to carry out divine retribution.

However, after a week had passed with still no result, I began to be discouraged. When I get enthusiastic about something I can sit up all night working, but, being impetuous by nature, my enthusiasm for anything I've set my hand to has never lasted long. Even though I was supposed to be the avenging right arm of Heaven, I still got bored.

By the sixth night I was a little restless. On the seventh I wanted to stay at home. Hotta, on the other hand, was obstinacy itself. He would sit with his eye glued to the peephole from early evening until after midnight, staring at the area beneath the round gas lamp that hung outside the Kadoya. When I arrived he would surprise me with such statistics as how many customers there had been that day, how many of them had stayed the night, and how many of them had been women. If I chanced to remark that it didn't look as though Redshirt would come, he'd say, "He'll come, all right," but would sometimes fold his arms and heave a sigh. I felt sorry for Hotta. If Redshirt didn't come Hotta would lose the one chance in his life to inflict divine retribution on him.

On the eighth day I left my lodgings at seven o'clock. I first went to the hot spring and took a long, comfortable bath, then bought eight eggs in the town. These were to offset the torturing diet of potatoes that old Mrs. Hagino subjected me to. With four eggs in each of my sleeves, my favorite red towel draped over my shoulder, and my hands thrust into the breast of my kimono, I climbed the stairs of the Masuya and slid back the *shōji*[7] of Hotta's room. As soon as I walked in he shouted, "Hey! We have a chance! We have a chance!" His face, which I've said before reminded me of the monstrous guardian god Idaten, had suddenly become animated. Until the previous evening he'd seemed to be moping, and even I, who was only a bystander, had been infected by his gloom; but seeing his face now I suddenly felt elated and, before he had a chance to tell me anything, I let out a cry of delight.

"Kosuzu—you know, the geisha—went into the Kadoya at about half past seven."

"With Redshirt?"

"No."

"Then it's no use."

"There was another geisha with her, but I think there's hope."

"Why?"

"Why? Because Redshirt's crafty. He probably sent the geisha on ahead and intends to sneak in later."

"Maybe. It's nine o'clock now, isn't it?"

"It's twelve minutes past," said Hotta, looking at a nickel-plated watch he had taken from his sash. "Hey! Turn that lamp out! If he sees the shadows of two cropped heads on the *shōji* he'll smell a rat. Foxes are always suspicious."

I blew out the lamp, which stood on a low, lacquered table. The stars threw a little light on the *shōji*, but the moon wasn't out yet. Hotta and I put our faces to the peephole and concentrated on keeping watch, scarcely daring to breathe. The wall-clock downstairs struck half past nine.

"Hotta," I said, "do you really think he'll come? If he doesn't turn up tonight, I've had enough."

"I'm not giving up as long as my money holds out."

"How much have you got left?"

"I've paid out five *yen* sixty *sen* in rent for the eight days up till now. That includes the money for tonight. I always pay my bill every evening so that I can leave whenever I like."

"That shows foresight. But I bet they were surprised here in the hotel, weren't they?"

"They're no trouble. What bothers me is that I can never relax."

"You can take a nap during the day though, can't you?"

"Yes, but I can't go out. It's killing to be shut up like this."

"It's a hard job being a divine avenger, but we can't let Redshirt slip through the net now."

"Don't worry, he'll come tonight . . . Hey, look! Look!"

Hotta's voice had dropped to a whisper, and my heart missed a beat. A man in a black hat looked up at the gas lamp outside the Kadoya, but walked on, out of the pool of light, into the darkness. It wasn't Redshirt. I sighed to myself. The clock down in the front office, with no thought for our feelings, struck ten. It seemed, after all, we were going to be out of luck this evening too.

Things began to quieten down outside and I could hear the drums in the brothel quarter very clearly. The moon peeped out from behind the hills around the hot-spring town, throwing its light onto the street below. All at once the sound of voices came from the end of the street. Since I couldn't put my head out of the window, I wasn't able to locate their source, but they sounded as though they were gradually coming nearer. I could hear the wooden ring of low clogs on the roadway. At last two shadowy figures drew close enough for me to see if I angled my head and looked sideways through the peephole.

"We're all right now. We've got rid of the one that was in our way." There was no mistaking the voice, it was the Clown's.

"Brute strength is no good without guile." That was Redshirt.

"That's true . . . Like the rough one that's always using such vulgar, downtown-Tokyo language. He's such a spirited, dashing young boy. There's a certain charm about him."

"You know, he refused to have his salary raised and wants to resign. He must be deranged."

I wanted to open the window, leap down from the second floor and knock the pair of them flat, but in the end I managed to control myself. Laughing, they both passed under the gas lamp and into the Kadoya.

"Hey!"

"Hey!"

"He's come."

"At last!"

"Now I can relax."

"Did you hear what that swine Yoshikawa called me? A 'dashing young boy.' "

"It was me they meant when they said the one that was in their way. Confounded impertinence!"

Hotta and I had to take the Clown and Redshirt by surprise on their way home, but we had no idea when they would come out. Hotta went downstairs and told them in the front office that we might have to go out during the night, so would they please leave the front door unlocked. Looking back on it now, I'm surprised the people who ran the inn agreed. Most people would take you for a burglar if you suggested such a thing to them.

At last two shadowy figures drew close enough for me to see if I angled my head and looked sideways through the peephole.

It had been hard waiting for Redshirt to arrive, but it was worse now, sitting there waiting for him to come out. We couldn't go to sleep, and what with having to keep staring through the crack in the *shōji*, and with one thing and another, I was all on edge. I've never had such a wretched time, before or since.

Rather than just sit there waiting, I proposed to Hotta that we should go into the Kadoya and catch the Clown and Redshirt red-handed. A word from Hotta, however, put an end to my idea. If, he said, we both went barging in now, the people at the inn would say we were rough-necks and head us off before we could reach the two of them. If we explained why we were there and asked to see Yoshikawa and Redshirt, they'd either say they weren't there or show us into another room. Even if we could get in without anybody knowing, Hotta continued, we didn't know which of the dozens of rooms the two of them were in. Therefore, he concluded, the only course of action open to us was to wait until they came out, even though it was boring.

We finally ended up waiting there, containing ourselves, until five in the morning.

No sooner did we see the two figures leave the Kadoya than Hotta and I were off after them. It was too early for a train, so they would have to walk back to the castle town. On the outskirts of the hot-spring town, cedar trees lined the road for about fifty or sixty yards, and to left and right there were rice fields. Beyond this, here and there, lay thatched cottages, and a dyke led through the fields to the castle town. Once outside the town, we could overtake Yoshikawa and Redshirt anywhere, but we wanted if possible to catch them in the avenue of cedars, where there were no houses, so we kept out of sight as we followed them.

As soon as we were out of the town, Hotta and I put on a spurt and came up on the two from behind like a sudden squall. One of them looked round in fright as he heard us behind him. It was Redshirt.

"Not so fast," said Hotta, and laid a hand on his shoulder. The Clown looked panic-stricken and seemed about to run for it, so I slipped round in front of him and blocked his path.

"Why would a man who holds the post of second master go and stay the night at an inn like the Kadoya?" asked Hotta, immediately on the attack.

"Is there any rule that says that a second master may not stay at the Kadoya?" replied Redshirt. He spoke in his usual polite way, but his face had turned a shade paler.

"You were so scrupulous that you said it was bad for discipline for a teacher to go to even a noodle or a dumpling shop, so how come you spent the night with a geisha at the Kadoya?"

Yoshikawa was looking for a chance to make his escape, so I stood in front of him and roared, "Who's a vulgar, downtown young boy?"

"I wasn't talking about you. I meant someone entirely different." The Clown still had the effrontery to make excuses.

Just then I realized that I was holding both my sleeves. I'd had to do this, otherwise the eggs in them would have been swung about when I ran. I shot a hand into my sleeve, drew out two of the eggs, and with a yell smashed them into the Clown's face. The eggs broke and large gobs of yolk began to run down and drip from his nose. He looked absolutely petrified and, letting out a cry of fright, plumped down onto his backside. He then began to call for help.

I'd bought the eggs to eat and hadn't put them in my sleeves with any intention of using them on Yoshikawa. But I was so angry that I'd hit him with them before I really knew what I was doing. Seeing Yoshikawa fall over, however, I realized for the first time how effective the eggs had been and, taking the remaining six eggs from my sleeves, I hurled them at him, calling him a pig as I threw each one. Yoshikawa's face was now covered with egg yolk.

While I had been throwing eggs, Hotta had continued his cross-examination of Redshirt and the exchange was now in full swing.

"Do you have any proof that I took a geisha to the Kadoya and stayed the night with her?"

"You can't fool me. I saw your favorite geisha go into the Kadoya early yesterday evening."

"I see no reason why I should try and fool you. I spent the night there with Yoshikawa. It's nothing to do with me if a geisha went in there yesterday evening or not."

"Shut up!" shouted Hotta and punched him. Redshirt staggered.

"That's violence," he cried. "It's an outrage. It's unjust to use force on a man without listening to the pros and cons of the case."

"Unjust or not, it's what you need." And Hotta hit him again. "The only thing a rogue like you understands is a good hiding." With this, Hotta continued to punch Redshirt.

Meanwhile I was raining blows on Yoshikawa. Finally they both cowered at the base of a cedar tree. I don't know whether they couldn't move or whether they were just dazed, but they made no attempt to escape.

"Have you had enough? If not we'll keep hitting you," we asked Redshirt, both giving him a punch.

"I've had enough."

"How about you?" we asked the Clown.

"I've had enough, of course," he replied.

"You're a pair of ruffians," said Hotta. "And what you've just had from us is a taste of divine retribution. I hope you've learned your lesson and that you'll be more prudent in the future. It doesn't matter how eloquently you defend yourself, you can't cheat justice."

Neither of them said a word. They were probably too exhausted to talk.

"I'm not going to run away and I'm not going to hide," said Hotta. "If you want me, or want to send the police or anyone else after me, I'll be at the Minatoya down by the beach until five this evening."

I followed Hotta's example and said, "I'm not going to run away or hide either. I'll wait with Hotta. So if you want to complain to the police, you can." With that, the two of us walked off briskly together.

I arrived back at my lodgings just before seven in the morning. I went to my room and began to pack straight away. The landlady was surprised and asked me what I was going to do. I told her that I was going back to Tokyo to fetch my wife, then paid my bill and immediately took a train for the beach. When I arrived at the Minatoya, I found Hotta asleep in a room on the second floor.

I was going to write out a formal letter of resignation immediately, but I didn't know what to say, so I just wrote the following note:

Dear Sir,

Due to certain personal circumstances, I am going back to Tokyo. Thanking you in advance for your understanding.

I addressed this note to the headmaster and posted it.

The boat was to sail at six o'clock in the evening. Both Hotta and I were tired and slept soundly. When we awoke it was two o'clock. We asked the maid if the police had been, but she said no, they hadn't.

"It seems that neither the Clown nor Redshirt has made a complaint against us," we said, and laughed hugely.

That evening Hotta and I left that wretched hole. The farther the boat got from the shore, the better we felt. We took a train straight through from Kobe to Tokyo, and when we reached Shimbashi station we felt that we were at last back in the world after a spell in prison. Hotta and I parted at the station and I've never seen him since.

I forgot to tell you about Kiyo. As soon as I arrived in Tokyo I went straight round to see her, without calling at my lodgings. Bag in hand, I burst in and called, "Kiyo, I'm home."

"Oh, Botchan! I *am* glad you came back so soon," she said, and tears ran down her cheeks.

I was so happy that I said, "I'll never go down to the country again. I'll get a house in Tokyo and live with you."

Not long after, a friend of mine got me a job as an assistant mechanic with the Tokyo Tramcar Company. I earned twenty-five yen a month, of which I paid out six in rent. Kiyo seemed to be perfectly happy, even though the house we lived in didn't have a fine portico. Unfortunately, however, she caught pneumonia and died in February this year. The day before she died, she called me to her and said, "Botchan, when I die, please, for mercy's sake, let me be buried in your family temple. Then I can wait happily for you to come."

So Kiyo's grave is in the Yōgenji temple at Kobinata.

Notes

1. The first man to open a photographic studio in Japan.
2. "Old ponds and frogs" is a reference to what is probably the best known of Japanese *haiku*, written by the famous poet Matsuo Bashō (1644–1694).
3. This is a reference to the *haiku* by the famous poetess Kaga Chiyo (1703–1775).
4. A *hakama* is a long divided skirt worn over a kimono.
5. An outer coat worn over a kimono.
6. Dark was an Englishman who took the first Western puppet theater to Japan in 1894.
7. A translucent paper sliding screen.